✳   ✳

W   ᴅ DEAD

The Ha⅄ Breed Gunslinger IV

While *The Half-Breed Gunslinger* fights for his life against infection from a gunshot wound, there are wanted posters being printed with his name and likeness. A $5,000 bounty on the head of Hunter James Dolin is more than enough money to attract men to the swamps of south Florida. The ending of the Civil War turns soldiers into bounty hunters as the North feels the need to cleanse the South, and men find ways to make a living.

The gunslinger's woman carries his child; Helen will need help from their close friends as her pregnancy progresses. Jebidiah and Walt will protect Helen at all costs with their experience and grit. Bodie and Bird, with their own skills, will be by their side in whatever comes their way.

To their surprise, unexpected rivals come after the newly named Dolin Family.

✳   ✳   ✳   ✳   ✳

[Artwork by Karlee Dawn 2014]

WANTED DEAD
The Half-Breed
GUNSLINGER IV

BRET LEE HART

Wanted Dead
Copyright © 2014 Bret Lee Hart
Sundown Press Edition 2017
Cover Design Livia Reasoner
Sundown Press
www.sundownpress.com

Prologue

The American Civil War was drawing to a close in the year 1865 and the structural and political reconstruction of the United States had begun. Four million slaves had been freed, but it would still take many years to gain any rights of equality under the Democratic rule of the South.

Following the assassination of the Republican president, Abraham Lincoln, just five days after the surrender of General Robert E. Lee, the Democrat vice president, Andrew Johnson, was soon sworn into office. His plans did not give protection to the former slaves which came into conflict with a Republican-dominated Congress.

President Johnson opposed the Fourteenth-Amendment, which gave citizenship to freed slaves; this began impeachment procedures against him in the Republican House of Representatives. This action against President Johnson by Congress formed the KKK from the Young Men's Democratic Club that offered a chance to take action toward the defeat of the Republican Party. The Civil War was over, but many battles between the political parties from the North and South continued on.

Florida was shielded from much of this political activity and did not suffer major structural damage in the Civil War, which helped to open up many areas of Florida for development. There were new players in the cattle industry, orange grove farmers multiplied, and timber production grew.

The Deep South needed rebuilding and Florida had the timber. Railroads were run into the panhandle for transport of logs and beef cattle back into the lower southern states. Black men laid track, some worked as cracker cowboys, and others picked cotton on the very same plantations where they were once slaves—but now, they did so receiving minimal wages. Racial inequality was far from over, but after 750,000 American deaths in the American Civil War, the path was set and change was certain.

Confederate Rebels, Union Yankees, Seminole Indians and freed slaves were thrust together all fighting for land, power and wealth. This was a recipe for cattle wars, fence cutting, cattle rustling, cow town duels, lynchings, and other vigilante actions. Lawlessness ran wild in Florida...and was usually settled by the gun.

Chapter 1

Lake Okeechobee, Florida 1865
Bodie and Bird had been sent to find Doc Holt and return him to the gunslinger's bed side. The infection that they had all feared had set in and taken hold. The bullet had been removed but the entrance to the wound was discolored and un-healing. Hunter had a slight fever and his strength had not increased since he had awakened over two weeks ago.

Helen cared for her man, never leaving his side for long, and she kept up a cheery demeanor whenever she was in Hunter's presence. They both knew deep down that there was nothing to be done, for infection was the number one killer of men in these times.

"Don't fret over me, Helen. You need your rest or you'll end up in a wood box next to mine," Hunter said from a sitting position upon his bed. He blew smoke from a cigarillo and then drank water from a tin cup.

"Oh, shush now," said Helen irritably, "we'll have none of that talk. Bodie and Bird should be back soon with Doc Holt and everything will be just fine."

"He won't come. You heard what he said—there's nothin' he can do."

"I will not accept that," she answered back as she tidied up the room and then went to his side to remove the breakfast dishes from the night stand table.

Hunter grabbed her wrist as she tried to walk away with his plate. "Look at me, please."

With some effort, she looked into his eyes as he pulled her in close for a kiss. "Thank you," he said.

She smiled and then crossed the room; she rested her hand on the door knob.

"I'll bring you some lunch in a few hours. Now git some rest."

"How 'bout you bring me some of Walt's Okeechobee whiskey," Hunter pleaded as he blew smoke from his nostrils.

"Yes, later in the day, it's kinda early yet," Helen said, and then smiled as she looked back upon him from the open door.

"Speakin' on whiskey, where in the heck are those two old coots?" Hunter asked. "I ain't seen them in days."

"I'm not sure. Jebidiah said he and Walt had some business and would be back here in a few days. Now rest."

Helen forced another smile his way while crossing the threshold and shutting the door behind her. She stood there in the hallway with her hand on the door knob as her smile faded, and she fought back the tears. She released the handle and rubbed the small mound that was beginning to form at her belly. Helen straightened up and wiped her eyes. With her shoulders back, she headed down the stairs.

□ □ □

The next day, Helen was in the kitchen cleaning Hunter's breakfast dishes once again and wondering when everyone would return. Jebidiah and Walt where overdue from wherever they had gone, and more importantly, Bodie and Bird had not returned with the Doc. She was worried.

Hunter had an appetite, yet she knew some of his hunger was out of sheer boredom; still, it was something. She had brought him whiskey the night before with his supper for she knew if she didn't, he would have left his bed and gotten it himself. Hunter's fever had jumped up a degree overnight. The back of her hand on his forehead could tell the difference in his temperature. She hoped it was from the whiskey, but deep down, she knew it was most likely due to the infection.

□   □   □

On the road, Bodie and Bird had tracked down Doc Holt to a small cow ranch where he was looking in on the pregnant wife of a rancher. They rode up just outside the house as the Doc was exiting the home. They did not have to dismount their horses to summon their request.

"Doc, thank goodness," said Bodie, somewhat relieved. "We need you to come back with us. Hunter James ain't healin' good, and he's got a fever."

"Boys, you wasted your time. I told ya there is nothin' I can do with infection."

"You got to try Doc, his woman is with child."

"I feel your pain son, I really do, but it's in God's hands now." The old Doc mounted his wagon. "Good luck. Yaw!" he shouted, as he snatched the reins and rode off without another look.

"What do we do now, Bode?" asked Bird.

"We go back, son, and pray along the way."

They turned their horses around and rode in the direction of Lake Okeechobee and back to the big house where the gunslinger was slowly dying.

It had been just short of two weeks since Hunter

had been shot by a hidden gun. Duke Montgomery had fired his Derringer a split second before Hunter had thrown his tomahawk and killed the Indian fighter. The bullet had been removed and luckily the lead had not hit any vital organs, but it was the infection that killed most men.

If he were gunshot in the arm or the leg, amputation would have been the cure—but Hunter had taken the shot in the side of his belly, leaving few options. Jebidiah and Walt had flooded the wound with whiskey while digging out the bullet, but the sterilizing liquid must have missed some of the bacteria that thrived in the swamp water. The germs had entered when he had fallen face first into the mud.

The only glimmer of hope was that the infection seemed close to the surface of the injury and did not reach deep inside the belly just yet, but if the bacteria were to continue to spread, it would eventually enter the blood stream and kill the host. A daily dose of whiskey on the wound for cleaning was the only option left.

Helen had just finished sweeping up in the hall when she heard the unmistakable sounds of pounding hooves riding in from the side of the house. Helen went to the big double front doors that faced the lake. A shotgun leaned against the door jamb. She picked it up and broke it open, checking the shells; satisfied, she slammed it shut before she opened one side of the doors and exited the home. Her Colt Dragoons hung from her waist and they were loaded and ready.

Helen walked out onto the front porch and then felt at ease when she saw that it was Bodie and Bird swinging down from their mounts. The horses were sweat covered and breathing heavy. Helen's heart sank, as there was no sign of Doc Holt.

"Where is he, Bode? Don't tell me you couldn't find him," Helen demanded.

Bode and Bird removed their hats and placed them on their chest standing before her with a look of shame.

"No, we found him ma'am. He wouldn't come."

"You took no for an answer and came back here without him?" she said with a scolding tone.

This was one time for which Bird had no desire to speak; he kept his head down, not daring to look into the eyes of this woman.

"Helen, what was I to do?" pleaded Bodie. "He's an old man; I just couldn't hog tie him and drag him back here."

"Well, what did he say? Did he say anythin'?"

"He said it was in God's hands now, ma'am."

"Sorry, ma'am," Bird said, speaking for the first time, fidgeting with the brim of his hat.

"Stop calling me ma'am, both of ya."

Helen took a deep breath and relaxed, she knew Bodie and Bird were loyal friends, and they loved Hunter James Dolin as she did.

"How's he doin'?" Bodie asked.

"His fever's up, he's sleeping a lot, in and out. He's gittin' worse Bodie, and I don't know what to do."

"You have your faith," consoled Bodie. "I ain't never been much for religion, but now is a good a time as any, I suppose?"

"Come inside boys, you must be starving and plum wore out. I'll fix you up a plate."

"Thank you much, Helen. That would be fine," Bodie answered.

"Thanks, ma'am," replied Bird.

"Bird, you can call me Helen; I think after all we

been through it's more than proper."

"Yes, ma'am—I mean, yes, Helen."

Helen gave Bird a big smile. The boy smiled back showing good teeth, which reminded her just how young he was.

"We will be right with ya, as soon as the horses are taken care of," Bodie announced as he replaced his hat.

Helen entered the house, closing the door behind her, while the two men led their horses toward the corral; they only made it five steps. Helen had made it down the hall when gunfire rang out from the second floor, six shots, one after the other. Helen froze for a moment and then she went to the door and swung it open to yell for the boys, but there was no need as they ran past her with guns drawn and running for the stairs.

Helen followed behind Bird as Bodie led. Bodie kicked open the door to Hunter's room and entered to the right, allowing Bird to enter and fan left, the barrels of their revolvers leading the way. The room was empty except for the gunslinger lying in bed and appearing to sleep. The long barrel Colt Walker was in his hand, and the room was full of smoke.

Helen came through the doorway sweeping the room with the shotgun; she looked over to Hunter to see his chest heaving up and down, sweat covering his brow.

Bodie walked over to the window directly in front of the gunslinger's bed and cautiously peered out; there was no sign of anyone. There were bullet holes in the wall and splinters of wood covered the floor.

Helen looked to Bodie. He shook his head and shrugged his shoulders. Helen went to Hunter's side and slowly removed the revolver from his hand that lay across his midsection. She handed the Colt to Bird who was directly behind her as she then attempted to wake the gunslinger.

"Hunter...Hunter James, can you hear me?" Helen shook him lightly; his shirt was soaked with sweat. "Hunter, wake up, please."

He opened his eyes with a moan.

"Hunter, what were you shooting at?" asked Bodie from the other side of his bed. Hunter's eyes cleared for a moment as he looked at Bodie.

"I saw him." His voice was weak but persistent.

"Who did you see?" prodded Bodie.

"The Indian fighter...he was after Helen...I saw his bald head, and his Montgomery eyes." Hunter's head turned side to side as he spoke. Helen laid the back of her hand on his forehead.

"He's burning up," she said with a helpless tone, "and now, he's seeing things."

Neither Bodie nor Bird replied, for neither man had the words. Suddenly, there came through the open window the far off sounds of pounding hoofs from many horses growing louder from the direction of the back of the house. Everyone in the room froze for a moment, and looked at one another as they tried to rationalize what was coming. The sounds of horses could be heard fanning out wide from left to right as the rolling sounds then stopped. Whinnies and blows from their snouts filled the air, followed by stomps.

Bodie, Helen, and Bird all looked at one another as they listened intently. Bodie was the first to react.

"What in the hell is it now?" He walked over to the window and peered out; he was speechless. Bird came alongside him and his mouth dropped before he spoke quietly. "Holy shit, Bode!"

Helen squeezed in between the two men to see what was there. She could hardly believe her eyes. Down below was none other than Sam Jones, Apayaka Hadjo Chief of the Miccosukee, and twenty of his warriors, all looking up at them.

"Well, it's been nice knowin' ya," said Bodie in a matter-of-fact tone.

"Yep, back at ya," Bird replied, with a voice steady, but quiet.

Helen looked at one man, and then the other, not believing they were giving up so easily. She was suddenly furious, for she knew these Indians; they were the same ones that dishonored her in the Big Cyprus swamp not too long ago.

Helen was wearing her Dragoons, but decided on the shotgun that leaned against the wall. She took several steps and kicked open the bedroom doors that led out onto the upper tier terrace.

"Dammit, Helen!" exclaimed Bodie. "Bird!" Both men pulled their pistols, and after a glance at the sleeping gunslinger, they followed her out onto the second story balcony.

"State your business," yelled Helen, with the scatter gun held at her waist, and aiming right at Sam Jones.

When the chief saw Helen, he spoke some words to his braves in the Indian language. Then, he spoke the words "leathers in mouth" in English and laughter broke out among them. The chief had given Helen this name at the time of their first meeting in a clearing on sacred Indian ground where Sam Jones had given Hunter the tomahawk. Helen had held the reins in her teeth, by Hunter's request, so she could keep both hands on her revolvers. The gunslinger had said some things about Helen that day to discourage the Indians from taking her as a slave for his safe passage. Hunter later regretted his words.

"Yap, yap, yap, like the Chi Wawa," the chief continued, with a gesture of opening and closing his hand like the mouth of a puppet. More laughter followed from the Indian warriors.

Helen's face was flushed red with anger as she cocked the shotgun's hammers back, one and then the other. She raised the double barrel up and aimed it at the head of the chief. The laughter ceased immediately, and was replaced by tension. The air was suddenly thick and difficult to breathe. Bodie cocked the hammer on his revolver with his thumb, but he did not raise it. Bird did the same.

"Easy, Helen," pleaded Bodie from the side of his mouth, not taking his eyes off of the Indians, and scanning back and forth, looking for any movement. "What the hell you doin', girl? We can't win this."

Helen ignored Bodie, staring down the barrel of her shotgun at the now stone-faced Seminoles.

"Not so funny now, is it?" said Helen loudly. "I ask again, what do you want?"

"We come for Lus-tee Manito Nak-nee," the chief said with authority.

"Well, you can't have him. Leave this place or die," she replied.

With this said, Bodie and Bird raised their revolvers slowly to back up her play. No one moved for some time. A bead of sweat rolled down Bird's cheek. "What are we doin', Bode?"

"Easy boy, don't do nothin' unless they do it first."

Suddenly, the tension was broken by the sounds of horses coming up the trail. Jebidiah and Walt appeared from behind the brush and rode in between the Indians and the house and stopping directly in the line of fire.

"Whoa-up there, little lady," Jebidiah pleaded, sounding out of breath.

"Lower them hammers, boys," yelled Walt, breathing heavy and grabbing his chest as he came to a halt beside Jebidiah.

"Oh, thank God," said Bodie, as he lowered his pistol. Bird did the same, but they kept their fingers on the triggers. Helen did not yield; she kept the shotgun aimed high on the chief.

"Helen, we brought them here," spoke Jebidiah. "They can help the gunslinger...it's his only chance."

"What are you talkin' about, Jeb?" asked Helen desperately.

"They got ways to heal I can't explain. I can tell ya Hunter ain't no better, or he'd be out there on that ledge by your side."

After a moment, Helen lowered her weapon and released the hammers slowly. Bodie and Bird took their fingers off the triggers and holstered their weapons.

"What in the hell is it with you two?" exclaimed Bodie. "You couldn't ride in here with them Injuns and tell us what the plan was, we damn near had us a shoot-out."

Bird chimed in, "Yeah, what in the hell, you old coots."

"We tried to keep up, but the chief, here, ain't much for waitin'," Jebidiah explained.

"Besides," said Walt, "I'm too old for this shit, so quit your squawkin' there, Birdie-boy." Walt winked at the kid and then took a draw from a bottle he produced from his saddle bag.

"Old coot," replied Bird with a small grin. Walt raised his bottle and winked again at the kid before finishing off the whiskey. The old man turned the bottle downward to show it was empty. "That's a damn shame."

"Time is short, Helen, and we done run outta choices," Jebidiah pleaded.

Helen sighed and walked to the bedroom doorway. She peered in from the balcony and looked upon Hunter. He had not moved, and sweat continued to flow from his body. He was not even aware of what had just taken place out back, not more than twenty-five feet from his bed.

"Bodie, Bird, can you help me git him down stairs?" Helen asked with defeat in her voice.

"Come on Bird, grab an end."

They carried Hunter down the stairs and out the front door to the side of the house where Walt and Jebidiah waited next to the wagon. Bodie and Bird loaded Hunter in the back and Jebidiah tied the Appaloosa to the rear of the cart. Helen looked at Jebidiah with a questioning look.

"When he's all better, he'll need his horse to git back here to ya."

Helen smiled at her old friend and walked to Hunter's side. He was unconscious and with fever, she kissed him on the lips delicately and rubbed his brow.

"You best live, Hunter James Dolin, for you have a child comin' that needs a father for the teachin' of many things."

Helen had hardly noticed that two Indian braves had climbed up onto the bench seat of the wagon. Without warning, the reins were snapped and the cart lurched forward. Helen walked after them a ways, and then stopped and watched as the chief and the remaining warriors tucked in behind and followed. She continued to watch until they turned the corner behind the pine trees and palmettos and disappeared from her sight. They were heading south, deep into the swamps.

Jebidiah walked up to Helen's side and placed his hand upon her shoulder. "He's in God's hands, now."

Helen touched her belly mound that was growing larger by the day. "I hope we're doin' the right thing Jebidiah. I surely do."

"Right now Helen, it's the *only* thing."

□ □ □

Three days had passed since Chief Apayaka Hadjo and the Miccosukee warriors had taken the gunslinger away. The old men, Bodie and the boy did not have much belief in Indian medicine; like most white men, they viewed it as superstition and folk lore and they figured the gunslinger would not survive the infection. They hoped it would be easier on Helen not to see him pass, allowing her to hold on to the thought that he was alive and out there, somewhere.

On the third night, Helen asked the men to join her around the kitchen table for drinks. She announced her plans that not one of them had figured on hearing.

She explained that one night where they had lived in solitude in the Big Cypress Swamp, Hunter had told Helen of his cabin left to him by his father. He had described the home outside Myakka City where the big oak tree stood tall and where the river forked. This was where Helen had decided she would give birth to their child. She would not live in this big house any longer. It was built by Richard Montgomery, an evil man that had murdered Hunter's first love, as well as an innocent boy, before trying to kill all of them.

Helen told her friends that she was moving on to where it had all started, and to claim the cabin that James Dolin had built. She would post a note, and she knew that Hunter would find her when he returned. Helen told them that she considered them all family and that they were welcome to come with her; if they did not, she would understand. She made it clear to them that her mind was made up, and there would be no one talking her out of her decision.

It only took a moment for all to agree to escort Helen home, at the very least. Jebidiah and Walt thought of Hunter as a son and Helen like a daughter; they would protect her for as long as their short time left in this world would allow. Bodie and Bird felt they owed the gunslinger for sparing their lives and rescuing them from the clutches of one Richard Montgomery. The gunslinger had saved them all more times than could be counted.

It took two days to prepare for the trip toward Myakka City. The remaining supplies were split up among the horses and a note was written on the side of the big house with dye from the Ink-berry that grew around the property.

Bodie yelled, "Move out!" as he led the way with Walt behind him, Bird rode at the rear with Jebidiah at his front and Helen was placed in the middle to protect her at all costs, for she was carrying the gunslinger's child.

It was an early spring morning, possibly April, when they left what was once Richard Montgomery's big house set on the banks of Lake Okeechobee. Not one of them would miss this place, for it was a constant reminder of the blood that had been shed in the war with the Montgomery family.

They locked up the three-story home, but anyone

could lay claim to it, for this was a lawless country. Bird was the last to pass by the message that had been written in large letters on the side of the building. His mouth moved as he read the note to himself;

For the gunslinger
Have moved on to where it all began
Where the river forks and the big oak stands
Loyal friends to the end
The Dolin Family

Bird could not help but notice that the letters written with the juice of the red ink-berry looked like blood. The young man found this fitting, for this place was where so many had died.

Chapter 2

Myakka City, Florida

The journey north and then west took several weeks, for their travel was steady, but without urgency. Bodie had led the way for the majority of the trip but now that they were days away from Myakka, Jebidiah and Walt would take the lead for the last leg of their journey. The old men had spent many years in the town of Myakka gambling and drinking in Matt's Saloon, and in the early days, the city had a family-run bordello. Walt and Jebidiah may or may not have spent some time there, depending on who was asking.

They knew this area like the back of their hands for Myakka City had once traded furs, salt, meat, and cotton for guns, ammunition, and supplies. The old men had seen the city of Myakka when it was first built, then abandoned, then burned to the ground and then built back again many times over many years. Jebidiah and Walt had no idea what state Myakka City would be in this time around. The last they had heard, their old friend Matt was now a tenant of the largest plot of land in the city, the graveyard.

They had more recently heard news that another old friend named Chuck Lamb, who had been the longtime owner of the trading post, had been killed by Duke Montgomery after interrogating him for information on the gunslinger's whereabouts. This was only a rumor, but both Jebidiah and Walt knew if Duke Montgomery was involved, it was most likely true.

Jebidiah was not surprised when the road that led into Myakka City showed little signs of travel, for the grass and weeds had grown over the sides, making the path narrow.

"Whoa," spoke Jebidiah as he pulled back on the reins. "Well, we made it. Myakka is just up that road."

Helen came around and rode up to his side. "Are you sure, Jeb? Looks more like a goat path than a road."

Jebidiah halted in front of two posts on either side of the road that were barely visible as vines had taken root onto the rotting wood. Before he could speak, Walt interrupted. "I got this, Jeb."

He groaned as he stepped out of the saddle and walked over to the side of one post and stomped through the vine covered brush. Walt dug around until he uncovered a wood sign; he flipped it over and rubbed it with a gloved hand to remove the dirt. It was worn, but it clearly read, *'Myakka City Pop. 60';* the six was scratched out leaving only the zero.

Thoughts of the gunslinger went through everyone's mind. Some recognized his handiwork and others did not, but they all knew this was where the revenge wars had all started.

"This is the place, right down this road," Jebidiah announced.

Walt caught everyone's attention with his loud grunts as he pulled himself back up onto his mount.

"Well let's git on. My backside is done with this saddle."

"Old coot," Bird spouted as he rode past Walt.

They all moved out one after the other, and in a short time, the overgrown road ended and opened up at the edge of the small town. They fanned their horses out and stopped as Jebidiah came to a halt.

"Welcome to the town of Myakka," Jebidiah announced.

"What a shit hole," said Bird.

"Back in the day, kid," replied Walt, "the town, here, weren't so bad."

"Everythin's 'back in the day' with you, old man," the kid spouted back.

"Well it sure ain't much to look at now," said Bodie as he struck a match and lit up a smoke.

"Come on, boys," said Helen, "we didn't ride all this way just to stand here and gawk. Let's git with it."

One after the other and in chorus, the clicking metallic sounds of levers and spins of cylinders rang out as they all checked their weapons, a practice taught to them by the gunslinger. Locked and loaded, they began moving forward at a slow pace, entering the town.

Helen tucked in behind Walt and Jebidiah, who rode side by side, as Bodie and Bird followed shoulder to shoulder behind Helen. They were on their guard and looking about, high and low, for any movement.

At their front stood a partially burnt-out barn with stairs that led to nowhere. They hung in the air two floors up with a ghostly feel. To their left was a huge dilapidated pile of scorched planks covered in green vines where the hotel once stood. Two plots down and to the left stood the trading post, weathered, but sturdy. The door was opened and hanging from one hinge. Jebidiah and Walt stopped, triggering a halt from the others. To the right, and directly across from the downed hotel, stood Matt's Saloon. They studied the second floor windows for a moment for anyone that might be lurking...a good spot for sniper fire.

Jebidiah spoke out while still scanning the upper floor windows.

"Walt, how 'bout you take Bird and check out the post and I'll take Bodie and Helen and we'll sweep the saloon?"

"I got a better idea, you three take the post and me and the kid, here, will take the saloon."

"Walt, this place has been ransacked long ago. I doubt there's a single bottle left behind that bar."

"Just the same, I'll find that out for myself; come on, kid," Walt said, as he headed the short distance toward the saloon.

"I ain't your *kid*, old man," irritably spoke Bird as he followed.

Jebidiah turned his head and looked from Helen to Bodie.

"All-righty then," he said. They all grinned at one another and took their steeds to the left, and moved toward the trading post.

Bird and Walt dismounted and wrapped the reins around the worn hitching post. With guns drawn and hammers cocked, they slowly entered the saloon by sliding past the open side of the swinging doors. Both bat wings had been latched back at one time, but the right side tie had broken, relieving the spring. Sunlight shone through the front door, casting shadows throughout the first floor. Halfway down the room and behind the bar, light shone through an open back door that lit up the staircase about halfway up to the rooms upstairs. The floor was dark, only shadows of tables and turned over chairs could be seen as Bird and Walt's eyes adjusted to the inside light.

The barrel of Bird's Colt led the way as he stepped farther in beyond the threshold. The air was musty and thick, which masked a slight odor. The younger man's eyes attuned quicker than Walt's.

"Damn..." quietly escaped Bird's lips.

"Yep, that's the smell of old death."

"It's not the smell I'm talkin' about you blind son-of-a..." Bird stepped behind the bar and began shuffling around.

"That a boy! Any bottles back there?" questioned Walt with enthusiasm. "Check them barrels—old beer's better than nothin'."

"Oh, hush up you old drunkard. Here."

Bird found what he had been looking for and struck a match, lighting the wick. As soon as he covered it with the glass dome and slid it down to the center of the bars counter top, Walt saw what the kid had been cussing about. Strewn around among broken furniture were dressed skeletons covered in dust. It looked to be four men. By the clothes that covered them, they were once cattlemen, cracker cowboys of these parts.

"Shit!" yelled Bird as he jumped and backed up quickly. Walt leaned over the bar and pointed his revolver to the floor where the boy was looking down. Another clothed skeleton lay there.

"I'd say that was once the bar-keep. By the size of that hole in his skull I'd say he got it at very close range."

The skeleton was resting on his back, revealing a large caliber hole through the bone and dead center right between the eyes.

"This would be the work of a Montgomery; a *Duke* Montgomery would be my guess?" Walt said, with a strong opinion.

"We best check the upstairs."

"First things first, Birdie boy."

Walt walked around the long side of the bar, bending down and searching low. He reached in, scraping the shelves. Walt stopped and looked up at the boy and donned a large smile. Bird shook his head as Walt pulled a dusty bottle, popped the cork and took a long draw.

"Is that all you think of, old-timer?"

"A bottle a day keeps the Doc away."

He took another swig and held the bottle up toward the boy. Bird stepped past the bones and made a face at the smiling old man as he yanked the bottle from his hand and tipped it back several times. Walt's smile was ear-to-ear, and Bird could not help but smile as he handed it back.

"Can we check the upstairs, now?"

"After you, there, young man. I ain't stoppin' ya."

They crept slowly up the steps with Bird leading the way. Both had a pistol drawn. Walt had a revolver in one hand and the open whiskey bottle in the other.

□ □ □

Crossing the road after checking out the post, Jebidiah entered the saloon first, followed by Helen, then Bodie. This had become the norm with Helen, surrounded by the men. At times, she was a little embarrassed with all the fuss, but she knew they felt it was their duty to protect her and her child—the gunslinger's child. Not for a minute did Helen think that Hunter would not return to her, but she was afraid to ask what the men thought. She knew, whatever they believed, the answer would be of positive thinking to save her from any doubt.

Jebidiah walked in deep enough for them to fan out and get a good look. The glass-domed candle allowed their eyes to adjust to the inside quickly.

"Oh, my," Helen whispered.

"Looks like signs of Duke Montgomery's back trail."

"I'd say your right on that Bode; this is for sure the Indian fighter's handiwork. Helen, you don't have to be in here."

"Please, Jeb. Really, after what I done been through..."

A board suddenly creaked from the staircase; all three raised their guns, putting pressure on the triggers.

"Take 'er easy, boys, and little lady," said Walt through grinning teeth as he moseyed down the stairs. They lowered their weapons at the sound of Walt's voice. Bird shot past him taking the steps quickly.

"There ain't been anyone here in sometime."

"*Someone* was here Bird—someone friendly to Chuck Lamb."

"What about Chuck?" Walt asked Jebidiah.

"The trading post is done cleared out, but the boneyard has claimed anew. We found his marker."

"He was a good man; unlike these crackers here, I'd say."

"You gonna share that whiskey?" Jebidiah asked.

"I'll do you one better than that," replied Walt as he went behind the bar and grabbed the bar-keep by the shirt. He dragged the sack of bones to the open back door and tossed him out.

Helen cringed slightly from the sound it made. She holstered her gun and sat down in a chair that remained upright. The rest of them watched as Walt brought two bottles from underneath the bar and thumped them on the counter top. He produced some glasses and began to blow the dust off. He began to pour as they bellied up to the bar.

Bodie had to slide a boned carcass with his foot to make room. Bird grabbed a full glass and dragged a table next to Helen, where she sat.

"Would you like a drink, ma'am?"

"Thank you, Bird. Please, don't call me ma'am, I'm not as old as a mother yet."

Walt continued to pour the empties like a professional bartender that had done it all his life, and actually he had seen it done his whole life as a patron. They discussed what they would do next as the night approached.

Jebidiah, Walt, and Helen would stay in the rooms upstairs for the night, and Bodie and Bird would take turns sleeping downstairs to cover the front and back doors of the saloon—but first, they would remove the carcasses.

In the morning, they would all escort Helen to the Dolin cabin to see what had become of it over the years. Whether it was occupied or broken-down, they would claim the land in the name of Hunter James Dolin and for Helen and the child that she carried inside her.

The men's first job was to protect Helen and the child at all costs, whether the gunslinger returned or not—and maybe, in time, Myakka City could be rebuilt...

Chapter 3

The wagon was left at the edge of the swamp and Hunter was loaded on the back of his horse for the journey through the Glades. A Seminole brave mounted behind the gunslinger and took the reins, keeping him from falling.

Pain lay in Hunter's side, and his mouth was dry. His skull throbbed heavily, and he was very weak. Vaguely, he was aware of his surroundings; he knew his time on this earth was short and figured the Miccosukee were taking him into the swamps to die as their Indian spirits required.

Before him, and through his mind, there moved a woman. Sometimes, she had one face, and sometimes she then had another. In his delirium he saw his past.

Lilith was moving in and out of his mind, and then Helen would appear. Hunter tried to think it out, but his fever was mounting. He saw a flash of the young boy, Zeke, lying peacefully in his bed with flames burning all around him. Hunter moaned in the saddle and the Appaloosa snorted and stomped his hoof in the knee-high water as he walked.

Matt appeared before him, and through his mind he heard him say, "Easy simmer, son...easy simmer." The father figure said this with his palms facing out and pushing forward. Hunter calmed and then slept, only staying upright by the arms of the brave that cradled him.

Chief Apayaka Hadjo was leading them to sacred ground beyond the big Cypress Swamp to meet up with the Yaholi, a medicine man of the highest importance. The chief knew the medicine of the Seminoles did not work on the white man, but only on the red-man's blood of the native Indians of these lands. If the infection was settled in the Indian part of the half-breed, he could survive—as the white man's medicine had done its part. If the swamp spirits found his soul worthy, the roots, herbs, animal parts, chants and customs would be allowed to cure the fire sickness—what the white doctors called the fever.

Over thirty days had now passed since Montgomery had put a bullet in the gunslinger's belly with a hidden gun, and it had been over two weeks since the infection had taken hold.

After blinking several times slowly, Hunter's eyes opened to a dark sky filled with stars. He was no longer on his horse, but lying on his back. A breeze blew steady and the smell of the wet outdoors was like coming home, a mixture of aromas were that of swamp grass, bog lilies, and marshland waters. His vision was cloudy at first, and then cleared enough to see through the pounding in his head. A bead of sweat dripped into his right eye, which made the man he saw slightly blurry.

The medicine man bowed down bending at the waist and stopping nose-to-nose with the half-breed at a distance of twelve inches. He blew thick, black smoke directly into Hunter's face. Hunter choked violently, making his head pound harder, and to the beat of a drum that began thumping in his left ear.

The night breeze blew harder, running a chill

across the gunslinger's body. He discovered with a swipe of his hand that he was only wearing his pants and he could feel his feet were bare. Hunter had barley recovered from his coughing fit when the medicine man bowed forward and blew smoke in his face once again. He hacked up what tasted like blood just before losing consciousness to the sound of the beating drum.

Hunter's eyes snapped open quickly to a dark sky filled with stars, and this time, there was a large, blue moon. He immediately felt that his fever was lesser than it was at his previous awakening, which seemed only a short time ago.

He was weak but more coherent. He turned his head to the left to see a silent deer-skin drum standing alone next to a modest burning fire. Hunter slowly turned his head to the right to see a well-built chickee surrounded by saw grasses. He was off the ground and lying on his back on what felt like a bear hide that covered a cot; he could feel the ridges of closely tied bamboo digging in his back.

Hunter slid his hand slowly down to the wound where he could feel moving bumps; he jerked his head up to see leeches and worms eating at his flesh. His first reaction was to swipe the wound clean; he tried this but to no avail for the blood suckers where dug in deep, so he pulled on only one slug but as he did the bloody skin stretched as he yelled out with pain.

A voice rang out in broken English, "Leave them be, Lus-tee Manito Nak-nee, they must be allowed to do their work."

Hunter released the leech and it snapped back in place; he groaned with hurt. He looked up from his bed to see the intense eyes of the elder Lower-Creek

Indian. His skin was wrinkled and leathered like that of a worn saddle, but the eyes were clear and deep.

Hunter had heard of the Medicine Men of the Seminoles but he had never seen one. They were loners and lived outside the tribes, only showing themselves when needed.

"Where am I?"

"You are on spirit ground in the Pay-hay-okee."

Hunter turned his head, closing his eyes and feeling a little sick, suddenly.

"Pay-hay-okee," repeated Hunter slowly. "Yes, the river of grass."

He turned his head slowly back toward the medicine man. When he opened his eyes, the Indian elder blew smoke in his face once again. Hunter choked and coughed up some more blood. After a short time, he recovered and caught his breath enough to talk again.

"What in the— Must you do that?"

"The Yaholi blows his breathe through the pipe to draw back the stray soul of Lus-tee Manito Nak-nee."

"Stop calling me that," Hunter demanded in a weak voice. "My black heart of revenge is no longer."

"The evil spirits use the white man's lead to enter your body to darken the heart...the Fubli-hasi comes—the wind moon. Sleep now, a storm approaches. I must seek the strong thunder medicine taken from the tree just after it has been split by the lightning."

The medicine man turned and walked into the darkness beyond the fire light. The last thing the gunslinger saw before he lost consciousness was the Indian's peacock span of feathers attached to his back. He recognized the quills, some from the buzzard and some from the osprey. Thunder and lightning cracked across the sky.

□   □   □

Hunter awoke at night once again to a star-filled sky surrounding the blue moon. His head was clearer than before, but he had no sense of time. He had no idea how long he had been here. He was soaked to the bone and he figured he must have slept through the rain.

His thoughts wandered. Helen was out there somewhere and carrying his child. He suddenly panicked and tried to sit up. Pain shot through his side, and he immediately gave up the thought of getting to his feet. He felt helpless, sick and weak. The infection was in his blood, and he would certainly die if the Indian medicine did not work. He looked down at his wound to see the leeches sucking his blood and the maggots eating his flesh; it took all he had to leave them be.

He turned his head and stared into the fire. He could not feel the heat, for it was too far away. No matter, for he had his fever to keep him warm. Hunter drifted into sleep...his last thoughts were of thirst.

He was awakened when the liquid touched his lips. Hunter opened his eyes to see the medicine man standing over him with a skinned bag of water. He drank eagerly. The water ran down his neck, cooling him. The Indian poured some over his sweaty forehead, soothing and clearing his mind somewhat. The Indian produced chunks of cooked meat and began to feed him small pieces, one at a time. The meat was tender and delicious; it was nothing like he had ever had.

"What is this meat?" he asked.

"From the cow of the sea that travels the rivers."

"The sea cow, Manatee...I have not had this since I was a youngster. I had forgotten. Thank you...what do I call you?"

"Yaholi."

"Yaholi? That means medicine man, is this right?"

No answer.

Hunter finished the small bowl of meat which gave him strength but made him tired at the same time.

"So what's the plan, Yaholi? Will I live?" Hunter asked, intending to hear the worst, for he figured there was no way out but one, for all the men that he had killed would soon rise from the dead and come for him to seek their revenge.

"Soon, the wind moon will rise. The night of the Fubli-hasi will cover the swamp with a mist swallowing the Pay-hay-okee. The river of grass will be the battle ground between the evil spirit and the spirit of good. They will fight over the soul of Lus-tee Manito Nak-nee. Now, drink."

The medicine man poured a black liquid into his mouth from a halved coconut shell. The fluid was thick and bitter and went down hard. More smoke was blown in his face and when his coughing fit was done, the old Indian began to chant and dance around the gunslinger as the drum began to beat. Hunter turned his head to see through blurry vision that the fire had grown and a single Indian warrior played the drum. *Where did he come from?*

There were trails of colors coming from the drummer's hands as they moved up and down in a slow motion and the flames from the growing fire flickered eerily. Everything was moving in brilliance and seemed to be alive. The medicine man made another pass in his sight and the spread of feathers on his back moved independently.

Hunter suddenly felt pain in his side; he looked down to see the Yaholi cutting away the leeches from his wound and throwing them into the fire. The worms were swiped away with a quill taken from the wing of a buzzard.

The old Indian spoke as he worked; his voice sounded as if he was speaking under water.

"The war medicine will summon the spirits, good and evil." The Yaholi scooped a silver colored powder from a buckskin bag and applied it to the infected flesh with the black feather.

"Dream, half-breed; in the night, the ghost goes north and then east, but comes back before dawn. The sick body shakes."

Hunter's eyes closed and his body began to shake uncontrollably.

The medicine man's chants became louder as he sang in an ancient Indian language, calling the ghost back from the east to the middle-south. *If the ghost comes back, the body gets well. It takes four days to avoid death, dream, sickness, and death. If the ghost continues on to the east, death will come.*

Hunter lost consciousness to the song of the ghost dance as a mist overtook the swamp, setting the battle for the half-breed's soul.

Chapter 4

Hunter awoke drenched in sweat but with a clear mind. The morning sun was shining and bright and he had to squint as he slowly opened his eyes. He was surprised when he sat up that his strength had returned and his fever was gone. He slid his hand down to his side to feel the scarring of his wound. There was no pain and the color was good as the skin had done its job sealing up the once-infected bullet hole.

To his right stood the empty chickee looking old and abandoned, and to his left were very few coals of a fire long extinguished. Hunter was alone in the middle of the deepest part of what he thought was the Big Cypress Swamp.

Hunter eased himself off the bamboo cot and tried his strength by standing. He felt surprisingly good, considering. The medicine man was long gone. Hunter soon noticed "long gone" was also his hat, boots, and weapons; he was left with nothing but his pants.

Hunter looked to the sun for directions on which way to go. His only choice was to walk among the ankle-high water through knee-high grasses for what looked to be three miles to the edge where the forest began. North was his direction to Lake Okeechobee, and to the big house where Helen and the boys must be. Hunter thought of Helen and the child she carried; how long had he been here? The days were still cool when he had been bedded down in the big house, but now the days where hot and humid, the difference from spring to summer.

□   □   □

He left the dry raised hammock behind for the wet ground of the river of grass and began to walk. He bent down and cleared bugs and floating dirt from the top of the water and sipped ten handfuls of the warm liquid to cure his dry mouth. His stomach heaved a little, telling him he needed food desperately. He had lost weight and knew he must eat soon if he were to make it to where he was going.

If only he had his bowie knife, or a horse... He wondered if Zeke was safe and sound, and missed him more than ever. He drudged along wearing nothing but his black pants made of denim, the strongest fabric known to man. An osprey chirped high overhead with a mullet in his talons. Hunter watched it pass by and his stomach growled loudly. He needed food badly and pictured in his mind the fish that the big bird held cooking over a fire; he then pictured the osprey cooking next to his fish. His mouth watered, and he swore he could smell fired meat as his mind created the aroma, perhaps to keep him moving forward.

A water bandit crossed his path, spooked by the sloshing of his feet through the marsh water. Hunter chased the snake as it swam faster; he reached down and grabbed it by the tail. The snake struck at his hand hitting nothing but air; Hunter struck back with his other hand and snatched the two foot snake at the back of its neck, and with one swift jerk, he separated the head from its body. It took a minute for the nerves to calm as it wiggled around. He had to force himself not to take a bite of the moving reptile, his appetite was so great. To be this hungry, he must have not eaten for over a week. He looked to the woods that were closer now, and he thought of what he would need to start a fire. He would make himself wait a little longer for his nourishment. With the snake in his clutches, he continued on toward the thicket with purpose.

The gunslinger climbed the bank at the edge of the woods lined with cypress trees and an occasional pine, giving a large gator that was sunning on the rim a wide berth. If only he had his bowie knife, he would spend the last of his energy thrusting the blade at the nape of the reptile's thick neck.

Moving forward deeper onto dry land, he tucked the snake halfway into his pant line and began searching for dry leaves, moss, twigs and sticks and a dry, flat spot for a fire. He found some loose lime rock stones and used their sharp edge to cut several lengths of vine against the trunk of a tree. He dug around the ground till he found a branch with a bend in it like an elbow, and snapped it to length with his knee.

A downed pine tree supplied the board of bark with deadwood on its inside for the drilling. He made the bow by tying the fibrous vine on each end of the bent branch that was as long as his arm and thick as his middle finger. There was enough slack in the vine to make one wrap around a selected stick the size of an arrow for the quick turning to create the friction. With the bark side down and the wood side up of the pine board, he began to drill a hole with a sawing motion, faster and faster, until it began to smoke.

He stopped for a moment and dropped pinches of

dry moss around the end of the stick, and began to saw again. More smoke was fashioned, as the friction created heat from the quick motion; Hunter blew on it, continuing to saw and spin the arrow-shaped stick back and forth. When he broke through the board of bark, air from underneath ignited a small flame which appeared out of another puff of smoke.

He added some dry leaves and twigs, feeding the flames, and then took bigger sticks and made a tee-pee over the top.

Hunter's fingernails had grown long, helping him to skin the snake without his blade. He peeled the skin at the neck all the way around from the meat until he could get a good hold of it and pulled toward the tail, separating the skin all at once in one large peel. He would not take the time to make a spit and he laid the snake on the sticks directly into the fire.

After a minute, the smell of the cooking meat made his mouth water. He reached in and flipped the snake once and waited as long as he could before pulling it out. The meat was rare, but delicious, as he devoured it down and around the bones.

Hunter made his way back to the water's edge and drank until he could drink no more; the meat revived him, but would not last, for he had a long way to go on foot. On his way back to the fire, he spotted a patch of swamp grapes. He wondered how he had missed them. He figured he was focused on cooking the snake meat creating a sort of tunnel-vision. He ate many grapes until he was full, and filled some elephant ear leaves with a supply for the journey north. He then broke off some grape vines the length of his fingers and returned to the fire. *It weren't to-bacco, but it would have to do...* After chain-smoking two of the sticks, he carried his pouch of grapes and headed north through the woods to find his friends and the woman that held his heart and carried his child.

Chapter 5

The Dolin Family had made the two-hour journey to the cabin marked by the big oak at the fork of the river. The cabin that James Dolin, the father of Hunter, had built. The dwelling seemed unoccupied from a distance, but they only found out for sure after Bodie had kicked the door in. Bird followed him in with guns drawn as they stepped down inside. The dust and dirt was thick, especially around an open window where the shutter had blown open.

The sun shone through the closed shutters in patterns of yellow crosses of light. Helen was pleased to see the crosses shining around the room, not realizing the cross-cut slits in the shutters were for shooting out of in a defensive stand, and not for religious purposes. Jeb figured what she was thinking by her look, and he hoped she would never have to realize the true making of them.

Bodie and Bird opened all the shutters to lighten the sunken room for a better look, and Walt began his search for any whiskey bottles left behind. A whistle blew, off in the distance, from a steam ship traveling the river.

Helen barely noticed, for she had found a broom and began to brush cobwebs and sweep toward the open door.

"I'll go take a look at the barn," announced Bodie. "You comin' with, Bird?"

"Sure, Bode."

Helen was sweeping around an overturned chair as Walt reached down for it and turned it upright.

"Thank you, Walt," said Helen.

"What fer?" asked Walt as he sat down in the chair in that exact spot.

Helen stopped sweeping, looked down at him and made a face.

"You old dummy!" spouted Jebidiah. "Move the dang chair out the way; the woman's workin'."

"Alright, alright, I just was takin' a load off for a dang minute."

"Come on Walt, let's check on the corral and the fences; I'd seen a few posts down on the way in."

"You check the posts, I'm gonna check that outhouse at the back before there's a real mess to clean up."

"Oh, Walt," said Helen, making a worse face then before. She continued cleaning with a smile as the old coots could be heard bickering out the door and into the yard. Stopping for a minute, and all alone now, Helen looked around the room, and she then turned sad.

"Where are you, Hunter James Dolin?" she spoke aloud. After a pause, a deep breath, and a sigh, she went back to her work and pushed her sadness from her mind.

The house and the barn were in good shape and it did not take long to clean and fix up odds and ends around the property.

□ □ □

After two days of work, Jebidiah and Walt had tracked down and killed a hog feeding on the roots of wild palmettos that grew in abundance across the river. The old men had dug a pit and slow-cooked the pig on a spit with a wood box over top to hold the smoke.

Helen had sent Bird out to round up a mess of swamp cabbage—not far from the cabin were a stretch of young sable palms, or cabbage palms that grew like weeds in these parts. He had to chop down several small trees to get to the heart of the palm for enough to feed them all. Helen boiled up the cabbage hearts with fat back carved from the pig for flavor, and to her delight, Bird had brought her a sack cloth full of wild onions he had found on his return. They sat on the front porch, feasting and drinking the whiskey brought with them from Matt's Saloon as they discussed what they would do next.

"While I got y'all in one place," said Helen, "I'd like to thank you for your help and hard work; I appreciate it, and I think of y'all as family. I know Hunter would feel the same."

The gunslinger, to this point, had not been mentioned out loud in sometime, and when Helen spoke his name, the men looked away or sipped their tin of whiskey or coffee. Helen saw their discomfort and their silence said much.

"I know y'all don't believe he will return, but I know he is alive; my faith and heart tells me so."

After a moment of uncomfortable silence, Jebidiah spoke up.

"You be right, Helen. If anyone...well, he's the Half-Breed Gunslinger—"

Walt then interrupted Jebidiah, as was his usual way.

"I been walkin' above ground for a long time and that half-breed is the toughest son-of-a-...gun I ever did see. He will find you, little lady."

"You old coot," Bird whispered into his tin. Walt gave him the evil eye but before he could shoot back, Helen continued.

"This place is sound as a dollar and will be a good place to birth our child. I still have a few months, and I heard y'all talkin' about rebuildin' Myakka...is that the plan?"

Bodie looked to Jebidiah and Walt; they gave him the floor. He stepped a little forward and took a puff off his cigarillo.

"Well, ma'am, with the cattlemen moving more and more south, we figure that town could be boomin' once again. Me and the boy, here, were thinkin' on buildin' the hotel back, and Jeb and Walt could get Matt's place back up and runnin'. We could hire a local to run the tradin' post; there's plenty of Mont-gomery gold left for the rebuildin'."

"When do we leave?" Helen asked.

"With the risin' of the sun," said Jebidiah. "If that be right with you, little lady?"

Helen nodded with a smile.

"Hot damn!" yelped Walt. "That calls for a drink."

They drank and they ate, smoked, and laughed, telling stories of The Half-Breed Gunslinger through the night. Every time the old men told the stories of Hunter James Dolin, the tales grew more wondrous with every drink. Through all their celebration and smiles, deep down underneath, the men knew they would never see the gunslinger again; only Helen believed he would return.

Out of respect, the men would continue keeping their thoughts to themselves, allowing Helen to keep her hopes and dreams alive.

Chapter 6

Hunter had traveled the high ground when at all possible. He rationed out the wild grapes for as long as he could until he was forced to hunt. The urgency to find his friends pushed him forward but the constant search for food was slowing him down greatly. He set up camp near some rabbit trails that he had found one early morning in some grassy meadows strewn throughout the thicket. He built three snare traps out of sight from where he slept and then played the waiting game.

Cotton tails traveled the same paths as were their nature and would ensnare themselves in the hanging vines set up by the trapper, strangling themselves in their attempt to get away. Two out of the three snares trapped three rabbits in a four-day period, two in the morning and one in the evening, which were their preferred feeding times.

Hunter had saved the bow for making fire and collected new woods for cooking the meat. He ate the largest of the three and rationed the rest for his long journey to keep him moving forward until he would have to stop and hunt again. He stretched out the rabbit meat for four days and made some good travel time.

Now, a week later, the rabbit meat was long gone and he was starving once again. On the search for food, Hunter found through thick woods, that no man had ever traveled, a patch of thorny black berries that he gorged himself on until he crashed into a sleep. He had used palm fronds and elephant ears for blankets during the night, not for warmth but to keep the mosquitoes from eating him alive. He woke three hours before the sun, itching insect bites that were numerous covering his bare chest and shoulders. Hunter was angry with himself for acting like a greenhorn and falling asleep without protecting himself.

Travel in the dark was slow, but soon the hot Florida sun had him sweating and moving faster, scratching his bug bites like a mutt covered with fleas. He moved on, cussing the Indians that left him in the wilderness with nothing but his pants.

Hunter kept moving north using the sun as his marker when he suddenly stopped to listen. He heard the sound of moving water. He had been traveling high ground for some time, and the only source of water were pockets of early morning dew cupped in the leaves of plants for the rains had not come. Hunter left the easier travel of the grass and headed for the thick woods of vine covered Oak and Cypress trees toward the rushing sound.

Breaking through the brush, he discovered a spring-fed river. It was shallow, with pockets of depth, as well as crystal clear. He walked straight into the water to his thighs and dove in; the water was refreshing and cold as ice. He came up and out with a yell and made his way back to the bank at a sunny spot to warm himself on the shore. He cupped handfuls of water until his thirst was quenched.

Watching bluegills swim by made his stomach growl as he pictured them cooking over a fire; he could smell the sweet flaky meat as he thought more about it. He began to ponder his state of affairs as the cold water cleared his head.

If you're gonna get out of these woods alive, half-breed, and find your way back to Helen, you've got to start thinking like an Indian. You have relied on steel and gunpowder for too long.

He began to study the shoreline where he saw pockets of jutting lime rocks breaking through the sand and mud that were covered with brown tree leaves.

You need sharp rock, half-breed. Flint, you need flint.

Hunter looked down and to his right and there it was, just below the water line, small pieces of rounded rock—but with the distinct edges of flint rock. He pulled several choice pieces from the sand and used one to shape the other by slamming and chipping away until he had a point on one side and a flattened spot on the other. He took his time as he taught himself this new craft, relying only on his childhood memories and of stories told.

A school of alligator gar swam by; the smallest of them were two feet in length, setting him at a faster pace to his work. Satisfied he had shaped a good spear head, he headed up the bank in search of vine and a straight tree branch of the right width.

Using the spearhead, he chipped away at the base of a small pepper tree, then broke it at a six-foot length. The branch had good weight and thickness and was very straight; he notched out the center of one end with the flint which reminded him again he was without his knife.

It took some time but soon the long, narrow, flat side of the flint head fit tightly in between the two pieces of wood outside the cut. Using selected pieces of vine and wishing for rawhide, Hunter wrapped the end tight around and around again until the flint became one with the branch and locked in place with the pointed sharp side out.

The spear was crude, but extremely deadly and had worked well for early man. It was not ideal for fishing, but was more suited for wild game or as a weapon, but right now the source of his next meal was swimming up and down the waterway.

Finding the materials he needed to make the spear had led him a mile farther north and inland from the spring-fed river. He collected his bearings and followed the trees that grew thick along the shore of the water source until he found a flat clearing along the bank, a good place to fish and set up camp for the night.

Hunter stood still up to his knees in the water and waited for fish to swim by. It was at the river bend and the current brought the gars' path directly in front of him. After a few thrusts with the spear, he noticed he needed to shoot under the target, for the water changed the perception of where the fish lay. On his fourth try, the gig hit its mark as the evening set in.

The fire was warm and the aroma of alligator gar cooking on the spit made his mouth water. He ate one side of the fish that night and saved the other half for the morning to start his day with energy as he continued on foot. With the spear, he would move inland among the palmetto bushes in search of hog. He had seen plenty of signs of rooting among the base of the palmettos in his travels among the high ground, but without a weapon, he would not dare take on one of the tusked pigs that were known to reach the size of a small pony. He made good time that day with his newfound strength and the thoughts of Helen, the child, and his friends who must think him dead. He had an advantage over them all, for he knew he was still living.

Chapter 7

Written records of days and months were not kept in the swamps of Florida. Paper was not widely available, and the thoughts of every day were to feed oneself. Farmers went by seasons, which were long here for planting, as the sun and rain were usually bountiful. There was no need for calendars where the weather told you what you needed to know, and the sun and moon told you the time of day.

For the first time in their lives, the Dolin Family had kept a mental record of how long the gunslinger had been gone and to the best of their recollection it had been somewhere around four or five months, giving little or no hope that he lived. In that time, they all kept busy rebuilding Myakka City, with hired locals and newly freed Negro slaves in search of a new life. Workers were paid in silver and Montgomery gold coin, and or room and board.

The hotel took the longest to rebuild and looked like the building of old. Bodie and Bird were the new proprietors and word traveled fast. Local girls who were made up of white, black, and Indian mixed were added to the gambling and drinking entertainment that went on at the saloon. Jebidiah and Walt decided to honor their old friend by keeping the old name of Matt's place. A sign hung on the front of the building that they all thought the gunslinger would appreciate.

The barn was rebuilt around the old stairs to the loft, the only part of the building that had survived the fire, and the trading post which had little damage was reopened. Jebidiah and Walt had known the first proprietor of the post, Chuck Lamb, for many years and felt it was only right to notify his family of his death. The grandson, Jimmy Lamb, showed up to claim his family's business. Jimmy had survived the Civil War, riding for the bushwhackers of the south, and had been on the run from the Red-legs who still rode even after the end of the war. South Florida was a good place to hide and start anew; he fit right in around those parts, and was good with a gun.

Cattle Barons were flourishing all across the state. Captain B. Hooker now owned four hundred and eighty-nine acres in White Springs along the Suwanee River holding nine thousand head of cattle, making him one of the richest men in Florida.

Jacob Summerlin, known as King of the Crackers, was believed to be the descendant of the first child born in Florida after the land was surrendered by Spain. Summerlin was a slave owner and a smuggler of cattle during the war, and at its end, he had amassed a fortune of fifteen thousand to twenty thousand head of cattle in lands from Fort Meade to Fort Meyers.

Track was being laid to ship the cattle by train to the north into the deep southern states to feed the rebuilders of those states, mostly in Savannah, Georgia, and Charleston, South Carolina. To the south, cracker cowboys were running herds as far as Key West, shipping cattle to Cuba and the West Indies.

With all the activity and capitalism creating wealth and trade for all men, slaves and Indians alike, towns like Myakka City were places along cattle routes to spend money on food, alcohol, women, and gambling. The freed black slaves were now making money creating more customers, and those who dared to enter white establishments were also free to be shot in these lawless lands.

The war was over, but tensions still ran high and everyone carried a gun. Many men became bounty hunters; they were men coming out of a war with no other way to make a living.

The Red-legs continued to ride for The United States Army hunting down pockets of rebel resistance, mostly in Texas and Missouri, putting a price on the heads of many who would seek refuge in the states farther south. Myakka City was up and running once again, and word had spread fast.

Bird was running the front desk at the hotel on a busy evening when a rider walked in with weariness of the road upon him. He was a tall man with tied down guns and the eyes of a vulture; his spurs clanked as he made his way forward. He leaned a rifle against the desk.

Bird was always armed with his Colts, but when he saw the man walk through the swinging doors, he immediately cocked the hammers back on the sawed-off shotgun that lay on the top shelf behind the counter.

"Room," spoke the man through his bushy mustache, as he slung his saddle bags up onto the counter.

"I got two left, one at the back and one up the front."

"One up at the front," said the man.

Bird pulled a key from the board hanging to his side, not taking his eyes from the man. The key had a wood plate attached to it with a piece of rawhide; the number eight was painted on it.

"That be on the second floor," Bird told him as he slid the key across the counter. "Staying long?"

"Don't know yet." The man took the key and dropped it into his top pocket. He began to dig in one saddle bag and pulled out a rolled up paper. Bird and the man's eyes were locked as he did this; the man opened the scroll and turned it around on the counter toward Bird.

"Seen this man here-a-bouts?"

Bird looked down at the paper; as soon as he saw it he knew his eyes had given him away.

"Can't say I have, but if you can leave this with me I'll keep a look out, let you know."

"Keep it, I got another." The man let go, allowing the paper to roll up on its own. He set two silver coins on the desk top. He then grabbed his rifle and saddle bags and headed for the stairs.

Bird was in a slight panic, and looked to the foyer for someone to watch the desk. Bodie was on a break over at Matt's place and he needed to go there.

"Amos, put that broom down and git your butt over here."

The middle-aged black man leaned his broom and scurried over toward Bird at the side of the front desk. Bird grabbed him at the shoulders and pulled him back behind the counter.

"Just stand here. I got to run across the street for a moment."

"Boss, you'd know I don't read or write. I's just clean up."

"Just stand here and stay away from that shotgun; I'll be right back."

Bird took the paper and pushed through the front

doors heading the short distance across to Matt's place to find Bodie, Walt and Jebidiah.

☐   ☐   ☐

Bird busted through the bat wing doors and bellied up to the corner end of the bar. Bodie was down the counter a bit talking to Walt as he was pouring him another. Bodie turned and saw Bird; with a look of irritation, he grabbed his glass and walked down to the end where Bird stood.

"What the hell boy, can't I git a break? You're supposed to be workin' the desk!"

"Walt, git down here," Bird said, waving his hand at Walt and ignoring Bodie's outburst. Walt walked down on his side of the counter.

"What's with ya, Birdie-boy? Look like you seen a ghost," Walt commented.

"Look!" The boy rolled the paper open and slid it to Bodie; Bodie looked at it for a moment and then turned it around and slid it across the bar to Walt.

"Where'd you git this?" Bodie asked.

"Some cowboy rode in lookin' for a room; he's up there, right now."

Walt read the paper quietly,

"Wanted Dead for Murder
Half-Breed
Hunter James Dolin
$5,000"

"This drawin' don't look much like him, but that won't matter none."

"Bounty hunters, shit!" Bodie exclaimed. "Bird, git back over there and don't let on that you know anythin', while we figure out what to do."

"Sorry, Bode, he saw my look; I think he knows already."

Bodie took a deep breath, followed by a long sigh. "It's alright boy, just be aware and stay alert from here on out; we been gittin' soft these last few months."

Without another word, Bird was out the door leaving Bodie and Walt with their thoughts.

"Hell, Bode, what the heck we got to worry over? The gunslinger's dead; it's been too long," Walt said with sadness.

"Yup, perhaps you're right, but I still don't like bounty hunters hanging around; it could cost us trouble."

"Cost us trouble?" Walt asked while backing up and bobbing his head like a chicken. "You mean like cracker cowboys, Injuns, Yankees and Negros all gittin' drunk, cheatin' at cards all in the same place, and all fightin' over the same women? You mean that kind-a' trouble?"

Bodie could not help but laugh at the old man, who made a very good point.

"I git your meanin' Walt, but don't say nothin' to Helen 'bout this. It will just upset her. The last thing we want is a upset pregnant woman with a gun."

"Look here, son—I was born at night, but it weren't *last* night. I'll give Jeb the heads up when I see him," Walt said as he walked down the bar toward some patrons who were belly aching for lack of service. "Hold your dang horses, I'm-a comin'."

Bird had crossed the dirt street and entered the hotel just as Jebidiah and Helen rode into town. Jebidiah had gone to the cabin to talk Helen into moving into the hotel as her pregnancy was nearing the end. It took some doing to convince her to leave the cabin, but it made little sense for her to be out there alone in her condition. Bodie and Bird had a first floor room set up for her to birth the baby. The problem was not one of them knew the first thing about such things.

Helen spoke as they walked their horses side-by-side toward the barn. "Jeb, you don't believe that Hunter is alive, do you? Not one of you has said it aloud, but it is as clear as the nose on your faces."

"I don't know, dear, but it's been too long for most men. Then again, he ain't most men."

"I see the looks on your faces when we talk of Hunter, and I do thank all y'all for protecting me from your thoughts, but I know he's alive...for if he had died, I would have felt it."

"I hope you're right, little lady." Jebidiah looked over at her to see her eyes begin to water. "I know you're right. If you believe, I believe."

Helen wiped her eyes. "I'm sorry. I don't know what's wrong with me."

"I'm just an old trapper, but with my years of livin' I have learned women in your state git a little more whacky than is usual, no offense."

Helen gave the old man a big smile. "No offense takin', you old coot."

"Come on, I'll take care of the horses. You'll be alright walkin' to the hotel on your own? They got a room set for ya."

"I'm with child, not a cripple."

Helen left Jebidiah at the barn and waddled toward the hotel wearing her guns lower due to her large belly. She was a great shot, and had killed before; now that she was with child, she was even more dangerous. As Walt would say, "More dangerous than a cornered pole cat with a hangover."

Chapter 8

The Half-Breed Gunslinger was gaining his strength and endurance with every passing day. With his new weapon, he had killed a small pig, and on another day, he had gigged river mullet schooling up in a bayou. He had taken the time to weave a poncho out of palm fronds to help keep the mosquitoes at bay. The worst were his feet and ankles that were covered in red, itchy bumps. He mixed palmetto root with pig fat, making an ointment for his insect bites. He worried about Helen and wondered about his friends, but right now he missed his horse, his guns and his boots the most.

The summer rainy season was marked by the afternoon thunder storms that popped up like clockwork. He traveled through steady rain and only took shelter when the weather was punishing. One morning after a violent storm, Hunter left the dozens of corn spiders he had shared a vine-covered pine tree with and continued his journey north.

An hour had passed when he stopped suddenly and began to gaze upon the landscape. He quickly realized he knew where he was for the first time since leaving the medicine man's limestone island. Hunter took off at a steady run. After twenty minutes at a steady pace, he found the lake where his and Helen's refuge still stood.

With the point of his spear leading the way, he kicked open the closed door and entered; there had been no visitors and the makeshift cabin, though dirty, was exactly as they had left it long ago. He went back outside and stared out at the lake at the water's edge and remembered the bear that had attacked him while he did his morning business. Helen had most likely saved his life that day by killing the bear that tried to kill him.

A bald eagle flew high overhead and called out to him as it headed north. The half-breed suddenly knew where he should go and what he must do, for in the back of his mind, he heard the beat of the Indian drum. The same beat used by the medicine man and the drummer brave deep in the Cypress Swamp.

Hunter found the clearing of sacred Indian ground where he and Helen had once been surrounded by Apayaka Hadjo and his warriors, the place where the chief had given him the tomahawk that had killed Duke Montgomery. The sun was setting, so Hunter began to collect wood for a fire. It would not be a campfire, but a bon-fire; its smoke would be seen for many miles.

Just before dark and after many trips with loads of wood, the waist high teepee shaped fire blazed in the center of the clearing. Hunter would keep the fire this way until needed, for he had decided he would walk no more.

To Hunter's liking, only several hours had passed before he heard the familiar whinny that he had longed for. From out of the thicket that surrounded the clearing came the chief and his warriors. Tied to one brave's horse was Zeke, who stomped and blew constantly. Hunter got to his feet and glared at the chief as he walked over to the Appaloosa. He stroked the snout of the paint and kissed him on the nose.

"I missed you boy. You have no idea."

All his gear was there—his Colt .44 revolvers hung from the saddle horn along with his side shoulder holster that cradled the sawed-off shotgun. The yellow boy rifle was in the saddle's sheath. He grabbed his boots that were sticking out of the top of one saddle bag and pulled the socks out. He began to put them on while standing and holding onto Zeke for support. Hunter found his black shirt in the same saddle bag and removed his palm frond poncho from over his head; the cotton shirt felt fine on his back as he fastened the buttons.

Hunter looked around at the Indians that surrounded him when he spotted one mounted brave wearing his black hat upon his head. He walked straight up to him and stared him down. The warrior showed no fear, but after a look to his chief, he handed it over by the brim.

Hunter combed his hair back and placed the Stetson on his head and turned on his heel. He went back to Zeke who was calling to him once again with a whinny and a stomp. He checked his guns while he spoke for the first time.

"Where the heck you been, Chief? You left me to the mercy of my boots; no, I take that back—to the mercy of my *feet*. No horse, no guns, not even a knife. Why?"

"The spirits have judged in your favor, Lus-tee Manito Nak-nee. Your Seminole blood needed cleansing to remind you of the old ways and to be one with the land."

Hunter was listening while he continued with the ritual of checking his guns; the powder was dry and they still held a shine. He strapped on the side shoulder holster and slid the scattergun into its place. He turned his attention back to the chief. That was when he spotted his bowie knife and the tomahawk on the chief's person.

"I will have my knife, Sam Jones? The tomahawk was a great gift, or are you an Indian giver?" Hunter immediately regretted saying this, for Indians lacked a sense of humor—but Hunter was still a little annoyed over the long walk.

"I do not know your white man's meaning. Now, go back to the fork tongues, and may your black heart heal in peace."

The chief tossed the knife, and then the tomahawk, which Hunter caught and slid into his belt. "Thank the medicine man for me, Chief, and may your tribe be blessed by the spirits."

The gunslinger said this as he mounted Zeke and left the clearing for the back trail running the horse hard toward Lake Okeechobee and Montgomery's big house.

□   □   □

The Half-Breed Gunslinger was complete once again. He was dressed, armed and reunited with Zeke, his oldest friend. The Appaloosa was happy to be back on the trail and running. Zeke had always loved to run ever since he was a young foal. The Appaloosa was a gift from the colonel of the regiment of the U.S. Army that Hunter had tracked for in his youth.

One day, he decided he was done hunting his own kind. That night, he rode off and headed home. Zeke was some years around ten and in his prime, and had been by the gunslinger's side through many battles, bad weather, and lonely nights. A man with a good horse was an elusive warrior or a brave explorer; a frontiersman could travel far distances high in the saddle—but a man without a horse was just a wanderer.

The Seminoles revered the horse and had taken good care of Zeke, but he had not run this hard in some time, so Hunter took stretches of cool down periods by walking in between hard runs and then watering with light grazing. The soreness in Hunter's legs was gone and he thanked the paint with wild apples picked along the trail.

During the walking periods, Hunter collected choice dogwood branches to make a bow and some arrows for hunting. The bowie knife made the making of the bow and arrows possible. His ammo supply was low and needed to be saved for the killing of men, if need be—and it seemed from the gunslinger's experiences that bad men crossed his path, whether on purpose or by fate.

The bow was quiet and did not give away a man's location like a rifle shot would, a cracking sound that echoed for miles when fired.

Hunter sat by a small fire, carving the last of five arrows, glad to have his thirteen-inch bowie knife that was older than he was, worn but razor sharp. He had saved some stringy part of the pig gut he had killed with the spear which he used now for the bow string. He had collected some dove feathers he found on the ground for the top shaft of the arrows, feathers left over from a kill by a red tail hawk. He identified the bird of prey by one of his feathers left behind when he had landed on the dove, talons first, at great speed. There were enough feathers for two of the five arrows that he finished; he planned an early hunt with the rise of the sun when the animals would wake to feed.

Tonight, he would sleep with confidence, holding his guns and having Zeke to warn him of any night time intruders. He had two more days' ride until he reached the big stilt house on Lake Okeechobee, where he hoped to meet up with his friends and complete a wholeness that he had been lacking for some time.

Hunter rose just before daybreak, and with his two arrows, he set out on foot to rustle up some meat. He wasn't sure what he would find, but the terrain was suitable for squirrels, or maybe even a turkey. The .44's hung from his waist, and the short-ened shotgun was cradled in the side holster for protection from man and bear; only the rifle was left behind. He checked his weapons as he walked, pure-ly out of habit.

The sun rose, fighting to break through a cloudy day when Hunter spotted a black breasted red peck-ing at the ground in a short grassy field. He leaned against a pine tree and aimed the arrow for center mass. The chicken strutted around pecking, and scraping with its feet. Hunter pulled back the draw string and held it for three seconds, and then he loosed the arrow, hitting the bird in the side just above the breastbone, missing the wing, and allowing the chicken to take erratic flight. He chased it down, and with a snake-like strike, he grabbed the head with an overhand position and spun his wrist, like a cowboy would throw a lasso, twisting the head off. The nerves fired and the chicken ran, headless, with an arrow sticking sideways through it and into the tall grass where it got caught up and then it lay to rest.

Hunter took his kill back to camp and stoked the fire back to cooking form before cleaning the bird.

The feathers were saved to finish the remaining three arrows quills. One leg, a thigh, and one breast would give him energy for the day, and the other half of the chicken he would salt down to keep until supper that night. The feet would be used for the worthy end of a good ole southern back scratcher, one to keep and one to trade. The chicken foot would stiffen over time, and tied to a stick, the nails of the bird could reach and scratch an itch out of arm's length.

Hunter ate quickly and then continued north with Zeke at a full run and walking in between for the cool down. Around noon, the thought of fire-cooked chicken crept across his mind and moistened his palate, but he would force himself to wait until his last meal of the day. Zeke was getting his legs under him and was back to full strength.

The gunslinger was back to full riding strength, and eating a mixture of fruit and meat regularly had brought him back to form; the pain in his side was gone completely.

Someway, he would thank the medicine man in this life, or the next. He dreamed of the Yaholi from time to time, but mostly, he dreamed of Helen. Some of his dreams told him that his once blackened heart was not totally gone but only held at bay, and only waiting to arise from deep within to surface when needed. He knew that the evil that men did would eventually find him, like always.

Night was falling and both man and beast needed rest. Hunter had ridden Zeke as hard as he could without causing damage to the animal, and here he had come across a stretch of ground that he had seen before. He relieved the Appaloosa from his gear and brushed him down with a brush with bristles that were made of horse hair. Hunter found this odd.

The wind was blowing hard tonight, making it difficult to start the fire with the bow. Finally, the flames were right for cooking, and he set the skewer of chicken over the fire on its spit and turned it ever so often.

He rolled a smoke from his diminishing supply of tobacco, surprised that the Indians let it alone, and set it aside for after his supper. He turned the chicken for the last time and headed for the woods to do his business, a certain business that would require a collection of select leaves.

On his return, he stopped suddenly; staring at the fire in disbelief, the stick of meat was gone leaving only the empty forks. He drew one Colt and pulled back the hammer with his thumb. Hunter stood perfectly still, listening for any movement in the darkness; there was nothing. He looked to Zeke who looked back at him with his long face. The horse had given no warning of an intruder...so what happened to his supper?

He went to the fire and searched the ground in the dim light. It took him only a minute to make out the prints he saw.

"I'll be damned."

He followed the tracks from the clearing and into the woods, losing them for a time and then picking them back up further into the thicket. There, in a small clearing, stood the thief finishing off his chicken dinner with a last gulp, stick and all. Hunter went to one knee but held the revolver ready. The medium-size dog spooked when he felt his presence, and turned, ready to run.

"Hey boy, how's that chicken? Good, huh?"

The dog gazed at Hunter with an untrusting stare, but he did not run away. Hunter stood up very slowly.

"If you want you can come along with me."

He turned and walked the short distance back to camp, not looking back. He planned to have berries and then a smoke for his dinner. He stopped and looked at Zeke.

"Thanks for the warnin'. You're lucky if I don't turn you over to the glue man."

Zeke stomped twice and blew in his defense as Hunter dug out the last of his berries. He sat by the fire and kept his eye on the wood line. After a few minutes and to his delight, he saw the dog break through the brush and lay down just inside the clearing; he was keeping his distance and licking the chicken grease from his snout. Hunter finished his smoke and fell asleep quickly; the last thing he remembered was the hoot of an owl off in the distance.

Early the next morning, Hunter and Zeke moved on, not pushing as hard as before. By mid-afternoon, they would reach the big house. They had a new tail this morning; the dog kept its distance, but followed regardless of the speed they traveled. In the daylight, Hunter could tell that the dog was a female, a chocolate Labrador, four to five years old.

She was a little thin and her hair was matted and dirty, clearly a stray for some time, maybe born in the wild.

Hunter stopped only once to take the time to split a coconut with the tomahawk at mid-day. He drank the milk and carved pieces of the white meat of the fruit with his knife; he was surprised when he tossed bite-sized chunks to the Lab and she caught them in her mouth and swallowed the coconut, chewing very little.

"It's not my chicken, girl, but clearly, you will eat

anything."

Hunter drank from a small spring alongside Zeke. There was room for the dog, but she was not ready to get that close, so he mounted up and waited at a distance from the water source. He watched as the Lab drank her fill, and then she turned and sat looking at them.

With a smile, Hunter turned Zeke with the reins and broke out into a canter. Hunter looked back once to see the dog following and keeping the same distance that she had before, running along within her comfort zone.

□ □ □

They reached the clearing just outside the tree line that connected to the property of the lake house. Memories flooded his mind, as this was a very familiar spot. This was the place where he had first seen Helen on the back balcony; it was the place where his attack had begun on Richard Montgomery and his men. In the second battle, this stretch of woods was where he and Helen had waited for Duke Montgomery's attack on them, and where Helen had been battle tested with her first kill.

The gunslinger dug through his saddle bags, glancing over his shoulder to see the brown Lab sitting at a distance and watching him. He tried another bag, and then the last one.

Yup, that figures, he thought, *them Injuns could not keep from takin' somethin'.*

His spy glass was gone. He wondered if the chief had taken it or if it had been one of the warriors? No matter, he would have no choice but to sneak in blind. Hunter checked his weapons and left Zeke loosely tied and the dog off in the distance to fend for themselves as he crept toward the house. As he crept silently closer with a cocked .44 in his hand, he could sense no one, and the feeling of abandonment washed over him.

He relaxed when he got closer and saw that the front door was boarded up from the outside and only the normal sounds of the woods could be heard. He holstered his weapon and meant to fetch his horse when he spotted the writing on the side of the house.

He read the note to himself. "The Dolin Family?" he said aloud. He kind-a liked that, but the important thing was that they were all still together. He cursed the moon for replacing the sun, for he was itching to ride, but traveling at night was dangerous and they needed rest. He needed to eat, but the night was only good for rodents or maybe an owl...then, he wondered.

Hunter walked around the side of the house and began searching the ground for the old men's stash. He found the door to the underground bunker under a mess of pine needles and oak leaves. He pulled the rope handle and slid off the top.

"I owe you a drink, you old coots."

The shelter was empty except for a small duffle bag hanging from a stick protruding from the wall of the hole; he reached down and yanked it up. He opened the drawstring and went through it. There was jerky, some tobacco and papers, a half-box of ammo for the .44's and a mason jar of Walt's Okee-chobee whiskey. Hunter unscrewed the lid and took several gulps before sliding the door closed and covering it back up to conceal its location.

Hunter considered sleeping in the house, but then decided against it, for he had gotten back to the comfort of sleeping outdoors. He would stay in the clearing away from the house and without a fire. There was no need to call attention to a passing steamer, renegade Indians, or bushwhackers that might be riding by in the backwoods.

Thanks to Jebidiah, he had jerky for supper and extra ammo, and Walt's contribution was the tobacco and the moonshine; Hunter managed a grin with this thought. He was sitting and leaning against a pine tree chewing on a piece of jerky when he noticed the dog was closer than she had ever been. Hunter chewed the dried meat loudly with his lips smacking, "Mmmm..."

The dog took a few steps even closer and then sat, licking the saliva from her jowls. Hunter tossed a piece of jerky to the dog; she caught it in her mouth and made it disappear.

"The next piece, you must take from my hand. You can do it."

Hunter waved a piece of the meat in the air.

"Come on, girl...it's alright."

The Lab's hunger was stronger than her fear, and in a moment, she came up to him and took the meat with a gulp. Hunter slowly reached out and rubbed her ear. She backed off a little from his touch and then, with her eyes, demanded more food.

"You need a bath, dog, even worse than I do; we shall have to work on that."

Hunter fed the dog a few more pieces, tossing them from a distance. She caught them in her mouth and swallowed as if it were her last meal. Hunter drank from his canteen and offered the dog some cupped in his hand but the Lab ran off to drink from the edge of the big lake. *Okay, girl, in time the trust will come.*

He bedded down with a smoke and sipped some

Okeechobee; his last thoughts before sleep were of Helen and his friends, whom he hoped were doing well.

Chapter 9

Myakka City was booming with activity. Word had gotten around very quickly that the cow town was up and running. Cattle drovers riding for several different brands made Myakka one of their stops for gambling, liquor and women as they drove the herds north and south for sales of the meat. Trains ran the cattle north to the upper states and to the south, ships were loaded with cracker Cattle in Key West and then shipped to Cuba.

Bar brawls were common in Myakka, from cheating at cards to jealousy over the working girls, and among rival brands, the cowboys often settled disagreements with their whips. Like a gun battle in the streets, two men would face off with the whips that the cracker cowboys used to drive the herds of cattle. It was said they could swat a fly from a cow's ear without breaking its stride. They would line up bottles on fences and compete with the whips, creating a whole new form of gambling. Walt and Jebidiah controlled the side bets and judged for a small fee, and for the most part, injuries were minor.

Cattle rustling were a growing problem, not just from outsiders but from the rivaling ranchers that fought for power, land and wealth. These rough men all drinking heavily and armed would often settle their differences with the gun. The town had no law or lawmen—only Jebidiah and Walt, with help from Bodie and Bird, served justice. Signs posted in Matt's place read: 'Take it to the street or be shot dead by proprietor.' If cooler heads could not prevail and trouble occurred in the saloon, Walt or Jebidiah had the right to shoot with no questions asked.

The saloon closed at three in the morning and opened back up at seven with a southern buffet of whatever was available. Bacon, steak, eggs, taters, milk and coffee were prepared regularly every morning by Bessie, a local Negro woman who had worked for Matt back in the day.

The cracker cowboys had moved on with their herds, leaving the town quiet. Like clockwork, in several weeks the town would be booming once again on their return from the south after the delivery of the cattle. They would be paid and looking to spend their money, and it would start all over again. In this last two weeks of business they had buried two cowhands, and one was sent home by wagon with wounds that would leave him lame. The wounded man was shot in the saloon and Jebidiah shot and killed the man who'd done it. The other killing was in a separate incident. The man with an ace up his sleeve was too slow on the draw.

Walt was enjoying the down time with a cup of coffee spiked with a touch of bourbon when a man walked up. Walt was an old war horse and had seen a lot in his lifetime. He knew a bounty hunter when he saw one. The tall man with a bushy mustache stood in the doorway for a moment watching over the swinging saloon doors. He looked around in every corner of the room before he entered. His boots boomed and his spurs clanked on the wood floor as he made his way to the coffee pot. His beady eyes locked with Walt's for a time, forcing Walt to slowly slide his hand closer to the butt of his revolver from under the table. The man poured a cup of coffee and dropped a silver dollar with a chink in a tin cup placed on the buffet table. He turned and sipped the hot brew while looking at Walt over the rim of his cup. Bessie came out from a back room with a freshly cooked batch of taters. She stopped suddenly when she saw the man with the tied down guns, for the older woman knew trouble when she saw it. The bounty hunter turned and looked at her. She continued on with her work.

"May's I scoop you some vittles, sir?" she said.

"The coffee's fine," he answered with a deep, raspy voice.

Walt was watching and took note that the man held the cup in his left hand, so any move he made would be with his right. Bessie glanced at Walt who flashed his eyes to the left toward the back as the man was turning his attention back to Walt. They were the only ones in the saloon, but the air seemed awfully thick and close. Bessie set down the cast iron pan and went back toward the kitchen, leaving the room. The man walked over in front of Walt and gestured to the chair across from him; Walt nodded in agreement. The man sat and they stared at one another in silence. Walt's hand was near his revolver but he feared it was not close enough.

"What can I do for ya?" asked Walt.

The bounty hunter set his cup on the table and showed his hands before slowly reaching inside his coat and pulling out a paper. He unrolled it and spun it around, pushing it forward to show Walt.

"Do you know the whereabouts of this man?" he asked.

Walt looked down at the wanted poster. "I didn't catch your name, mister?"

"The name's John Riley Duncan. Where's the half-breed?"

Walt kept his poker face showing, but inside his head, alarms were going off. He had heard of this man named Duncan, and he was not a man to take lightly.

"You're wastin' your time, bounty hunter."

Duncan pulled a gold piece from his top pocket and slid it to the middle of the table.

"I'm willin' to pay for information, but if you're holdin' out on me, well, let's just say I'm not a patient man."

"Like I said, you're barkin' up the wrong totem pole; the half-breed's long dead."

"Word is he killed Duke Montgomery and escaped into the swamp," Duncan replied.

"That's true, so the story goes; but he did take a bullet and the infection got him. That's the end of the story I heard, anyhow."

"Well, if you can't help me, maybe you can tell me where the woman named Helen might be?"

Walt's poker face betrayed him as anger shot up his back. *That was it!* He would have to draw and try to kill this man, but he feared his age would let him down. Both men knew what was coming and Duncan's eyes narrowed; the still silence in the room became loud as the tension built. Walt's life flashed before his eyes a split second before he heard the most wonderful sound he had ever heard: two clicks of the hammer.

Duncan's eyes changed as Walt grinned with relief.

"How are we doin' this fine mornin' there, Walt?" said Jebidiah, from his position directly behind the bounty hunter. He had both barrels of his twelve gauges aimed at the back of the man's head.

"Mister, you're more than welcome to stay the night, eat, drink, gamble, even entertain some of the fine ladies, but by mornin' you best ride on."

"You would shoot a man in the back, having a talk over a cup of coffee?" the bounty hunter asked.

"I'll do whatever I have-ta to protect my own. One more crossed stick in the boneyard makes no difference to me."

Walt had pulled his pistol and now set the cocked revolver on the table, pointing at the bounty hunter as he spoke.

"Who set this bounty, Duncan? The army? The governor?"

"No, no," spoke Duncan as he stood slowly with his hands up. "The army bought the story of the half-breed's death, but the last remaining heir to the Montgomery estate weren't so sure. I am here to confirm or deny it."

Jebidiah kept the shotgun leveled as he moved to the side and gave the bounty hunter the door.

"I hadn't heard of another Montgomery son?" said Jebidiah.

"Not a son, but a daughter," answered Duncan as his hand pushed open one side of the bat-wings. "Jane Montgomery, the most ruthless woman I'd ever met. Good day gentlemen, we will meet again."

Jebidiah watched from over the swinging doors as the man walked across the road and entered the hotel before he released the hammers slowly. Walt returned from the bar with a bottle and they sat down at the table.

"I'm gittin' way too old for this shit, Jeb."

"I hear ya, Walt. Did I feel it right? Was there a draw about to go down?"

"What the heck took you so long?" exclaimed Walt. "That was John Riley Duncan I damn near drew on."

"I know. Why would you try him, you old coot? You got a death wish?"

"He knows about Helen. He mentioned her by name."

They both drank from coffee cups that now held the whiskey.

"Makes sense," Jebidiah reasoned. "What he said must be true. Only kinfolk could know about Helen. Them Montgomerys have been a real pain in my back side like no others I can remember."

"You think the gunslinger's alive, Jeb?"

"I don't know. Helen seems to think so, but I just don't know."

"Where's Helen now?"

"Dag-nab-it! She's at the hotel!" Jebidiah jumped up and headed for the door.

"You best warn Bodie and the kid about what the heck's goin' on. I got the feelin' we gonna need 'em come morning," Walt yelled while Jebidiah departed.

Jebidiah had entered the hotel and watched the bounty hunter walk the stairs toward his room on the second floor. Jebidiah walked over to Bird at the front desk; he had a look of bewilderment on his face.

"Where's Helen at, Bird?"

"She's lying down in her room on the third floor at the back. What's goin' on, Jeb?"

"Me and Walt gave that bounty hunter the rest of the day and the night, but by mornin' he's to ride on."

Bodie came down the stairs from the third floor and joined Bird and Jebidiah at the front desk.

"Helen's gotta stay out of sight until tomorrow,"

said Jebidiah, to both men. "That bounty hunter ain't no run of the mill. His name is John Riley Duncan. He caused many atrocities in the war and ain't no one to trifle with. We gave him till sunrise to ride out-a town."

"I knew he was trouble," said Bodie, "but I had no idea. Helen's room is at the end of the hall, and for tonight, I'll take the room next door. She ain't gonna like being cooped up. She's already been complainin'."

"I'll talk with her," said Jebidiah, "but today we gotta keep an eye out—and in the mornin', we gotta be ready."

Bodie would spend the rest of the day in his room with the door open and watching the hall. Helen finally agreed to stay in her room after a back and forth with Jebidiah, for she and Jeb had developed an unmentioned father-daughter relationship since the leaving of the gunslinger. Walt was like the drunken uncle and Bodie and Bird were the brothers she never had. The closer Helen's pregnancy came to term, the tighter knit did the Dolin Family become.

John Riley Duncan ate his lunch and then supper in his room by the window on the second floor watching the street of Myakka. Walt and Jebidiah observed him from the front porch of the saloon, which made for a long rest of the day. There were very few locals in and out of town, and they did not stay long for they could feel the tension in the air that told that trouble was brewing. Walt and Jebidiah spent their day on the porch drinking coffee instead of whiskey, a sure indication they were preparing for something and it weren't good. They made it through the night without incident, sleeping lightly with one eye opened.

After a long, sleepless night for all, Duncan walked the stairs past Bird at the front desk with his gear in hand. Bird locked eyes with the bounty hunter as he went past and out the front doors. Bird let out a deep breath and released the hammers on the shotgun he held under the desk. His other hand stayed on the butt of his revolver as Bodie followed Duncan and stopped inside the swinging doors. Duncan stared across the street at Walt and Jeb who were standing on the porch of the saloon. He then looked to his right to see that his horse had already been saddled and was waiting on him to mount. With a grin and a nod, Duncan secured his gear, and with a practiced motion, he placed his boot in the stirrup and swung up into the saddle with the grace of a veteran horseman. The bounty hunter rode over to the saloon and stopped in front of the old men. Jebidiah and Walt rested their hands on the butts of their revolvers and the cocking sound of Bodie's rifle could be heard echoing from the hotel's porch in the quiet morning air. Their eyes locked for a long moment until Duncan spoke.

"We will meet again. Of that, I have no doubt. Good day, gentlemen."

With a tip of his hat, the bounty hunter turned his horse with a pull on the reins and gave Bodie a long look as if he were memorizing his features, on his slow ride out of town.

□　□　□

The Dolin Gang soon found out that locking up a pregnant gunslinger in a room for a day tended to make her moody. Helen had called a meeting in the lobby of the hotel over the morning meal to announce her intentions. She was coming close to a birth date and it showed; she looked to be hiding a large pumpkin under her dress. Helen still sported her guns, but the belt she wore was hanging lower and lower and running out of loops to buckle. They all sat at the large table and ate plates from Bessie's buffet. This morning's meal was a treat of fried catfish, grits and hush puppies.

"I will not be locked away like a sick patient. I am with child, not with disease," Helen spouted irritably. She stood at the head of the table as the men sat staring at their food as they ate. "I am a gunslinger and if my child is in danger, I will defend him."

"Him? How do you know it's a boy?" asked Bird. The rest of the men looked at him like he was crazy to be pushing this woman.

"A Seminole mid-wife visited me at the cabin. She has told me this because I carry the child high; if the belly mound was low, it would mean a girl."

Jebidiah spoke up, "Helen, we made a promise to Hunter that we would protect you, and that's all we're tryin' to do."

"I know, Jeb, and I thank you, but it was wrong for me to come here. I must give birth in the Dolin cabin; in a *home*, not a hotel for which the land was once owned by a Montgomery."

"Ma'am," said Bodie, "we have a town to run, here. We can't look after you out there at the cabin and be here at the same time."

"I know this, boys. That's why last night I sent for Alameda, the mid-wife. The tribal elders have pledged five warriors along with Alameda to stay with me at the cabin until the birth, and beyond, or until Hunter James returns."

The men all looked at one another, afraid to bring up the fact that the gunslinger was most likely dead and would never return.

"I don't like it," Jebidiah replied immediately.

"Are you sure we can trust them Injuns?" said Walt, speaking for the first time. "They believe the gunslinger is possessed by spirits or demons—that may carry over to the child. They may have other reasons to offer help."

"I trust Alameda, and I can handle myself. It's my decision—and we will be leaving this mornin' when the Seminoles arrive."

Just then, Amos ran in the room in a panic. "You best come! There's Indians outside makin' peoples nervous!"

"There goes the neighboring hood," said Walt, as they all stood from the table.

"Now don't y'all go runnin' out there and scarin' them off!" demanded Helen.

"Scarin' them off?" replied Walt.

Jebidiah quickly went into action.

"Me and Walt, here, will go on out. Bodie, you and Bird cover us from the window with rifles and let them see ya. Helen, git your gear; if your mind's made up, the sooner them Injuns is out of town, the better."

"Thank you, Jebidiah," said Helen. "Amos has already saddled my horse."

"You are one stubborn woman," said Jebidiah. "Alright, let's do this before someone gits trigger happy."

They quickly said their goodbyes and Helen rode off toward the cabin with the Seminole mid-wife and five Miccosukee warriors from the tribe of Apayaka Hadjo.

Chapter 10

The day was already hot and humid as mid-morning approached. Hunter James Dolin stopped Zeke and gazed upon the landscape. The stretch of ground was familiar, and he knew the cabin that his father, James Dolin, built was just off the path through the trees. He looked behind him for the dog as he patted the Appaloosa's neck.

"We're almost home, boy."

The paint stomped and blew in a reply, bringing the brown Lab from out of the palmettos and onto the road. The dog sat alongside Zeke and gave Hunter "that" look. Hunter dug into his saddle bag and pulled out a slice of jerky. He yanked a piece off with his teeth and tossed the rest to the dog who caught it in mid-air and swallowed it with barely a chew.

"You know, that jerky ain't half bad, dog—if you were to take the time to taste it."

Hunter guided Zeke up the road a ways and turned through a break in the trees and into the shallow creek that forked off the main river. There it stood: the great oak shadowing the cabin where he once lived. The place looked good, and as he got closer, he could see that there were some new wood repairs showing here and there. He was coming in slow and cautious, and decided to leave Zeke by the tree for now as he went in on foot. Hunter dismounted and began his ritual; he first went through the

Colt .44's and then he checked the sawed-off shot-gun that he carried in his side shoulder holster. He snapped the break closed with a flick of his arm and then decided to lead the way with the barrels leveled and facing forward.

He stepped onto the porch quietly, preparing to kick the door in. With a change of mind, he left the porch and went to the side window, peering through the cross-cut shutters. The crosses made of sunlight shone around the room from all sides, lighting the cabin enough for him to see that it was clean and empty. Hunter walked around to the front and looked to the barn. He glanced over at the big oak to see the dog sitting next to Zeke and watching him intently. This shaped a small grin on the gunslinger's face while thoughts turned to questions that went through his mind.

They were here like they said, but where have they gone?

There ain't no signs of trouble, this is good.

Myakka City, that's the closest place; best to start there, I reckon.

Hunter went back the short distance to Zeke and the dog waiting by the big oak. The brown Lab stood on all fours from her sitting position, but she did not run. He bent down to pat her head, but she dodged a little, avoiding his touch and then stood her ground giving him that look. He pulled a bite size piece of jerky and tossed it in the air; she snatched it up and swallowed the treat and then waited for another.

The gunslinger mounted, swiping his long black hair back and re-setting his hat.

"That'll keep ya for now, girl. We got to travel a stretch of road that seems to hold trouble for me, and you should be light on your feet as we do so."

They crossed the moving creek and broke through the brush in the same spot from where they had entered, setting out down the familiar road that eventually led into Myakka City. It would take two hours or so at a steady walk. Zeke could run it in a much shorter time, but that would be reckless, possibly coming up on someone too quickly. The dog would follow close, then lag behind. At times, she disappeared altogether, only to appear again from the thicket. Hunter thought of naming the Labrador. He wondered what the Indian name for "walking stomach" might be...

The sun was higher in the sky and it was hot when Hunter spotted a man on a horse coming toward him from up the trail. He had sensed their presence a split second before the man and his horse had come into his sight. Hunter decided to confront whatever came down the road head on.

Both men stopped their mounts twenty-five feet from one another. Hunter noticed he was a wiry white man with a face full of beard and signs of dust that could only be had from miles of travel. The two sized up one another without words for a time. They checked their flanks careful like not to lose sight of one another, in the case there was a move to be made.

Hunter noticed that the dog was gone. She clearly sensed danger and took to the brush. Both men took an account of the other's weapons. It was clear that two gunfighters had crossed paths and the decisions they made next would decide their fate. They were very careful not to make any sudden movements that might trigger the game before all the pieces were set in place; the gunfighters' game was one of blood and the loser's prize was death.

"Howdy," said the man with a raspy voice.

Hunter said nothing, but he did nod his head with a greeting. Clouds suddenly covered the sun making the world seem smaller and more confined.

"I'm lookin' for a half-colored man; he's wanted," the man continued.

"Are you a bounty hunter?" Hunter asked.

The man slowly raised his hand to show he wasn't making the move that both men were waiting for; he pulled back his coat to reveal his star, "Texas Ranger".

"You're a long way from Texas there, Marshal."

"He's...what do you call it? A ma-lotto. A runaway Negro slave. Goes by the name Darnell."

"I thought the war ended all that?" Hunter asked.

"Oh, it did, but as soon as Darnell was freed he stuck a pitchfork through his master's neck. As a free man, he will git a fair trial, and then he will be hanged. I got a poster here with his picture and a one thousand dollar reward if you might take a look?"

"No need, I know who he is, for he's a local. I haven't seen him in some time though. I've been far south."

"And what might you be doin' 'further south', Mister...?"

There was a long pause as the two men stared at one another. More tension filled the air.

"Doin' a little gator huntin'. Good swamp south."

"Gator huntin', huh? Well, I guess I'll move along then," the Ranger stated.

"I'll give you the road," Hunter said, as he cautiously moved Zeke sideways a few steps. The marshal tipped his hat and came forward. Their eyes locked as the marshal passed slowly by, the horses grunted at one another. Hunter turned Zeke around and watched as the marshal moved on. There was no fear in the Ranger's eyes; there was only wisdom as Hunter knew he had been sized up, so he was not surprised at what came next. The Texas Ranger turned his horse and faced Hunter at the same distance as before. They had switched positions. Hunter was now facing south and the law man was facing north.

"I got another poster here you might take a look at. This one is a mite better, with a five thousand-dollar bounty. I am sure you will know this man, as well."

They came at one another on horseback, riding the short distance while pulling their pistols and firing. Hunter did not like doing it dirty but he had more to live for now than ever before, so his first bullet hit the horse between the eyes. The marshal was dragged down with his animal quickly to the ground and the two shots he had fired missed Hunter, but by only inches. Zeke had side-stepped the falling horse as the distance had been closed. Zeke was turned by the way Hunter squeezed his legs at the horse's belly.

The Ranger struggled to climb out from under his dead horse while cursing, "You son-of-a-bitch!" He had lost one pistol. With the other hand, the Ranger swung around as he stood preparing to fire the revolver at the half-breed but before he could level it, his teeth were shattered in a spray of blood by the .44 slug that exited the back of his head. The Texas Ranger fell backward and came to rest on top of his unmoving horse. The game was over, and the loser's blood had been spilt.

The gunslinger did not feel joy in killing this man,

but there was some feeling of relief, for he was alive to continue on...to find his woman and friends. He dismounted and reloaded his guns as he stood over the dead man and his horse. Hunter felt a presence behind him; he turned while cocking the hammer. There stood the dog, wagging her tail with the expression on her face that asked, "Time to eat yet?"

"There you are. You did good, dog. Avoiding trouble is sometimes best. Maybe you'll rub off on me, you think?"

The dog walked over and sat next to Zeke and eyeballed the saddle bag that held the jerky as if she were guarding it. The turkey buzzards were already forming a circle in the sky directly up above, like a huge sign telling anyone who could see it that a kill had ensued.

Hunter went through the man's pockets and then rolled him off of the dead horse. He went through the saddle bags that he could get to and took food, water and any ammo he could use. He would not take the weapons, for they could be identified. It had been a fair fight, but this man had the law behind him. The Half-Breed Gunslinger had been labeled an outlaw long ago.

Hunter grunted as he threw the big man over his shoulder and walked over to the side of the road. He flipped the body off into the swampy woods in a spot where the water was deep. He cut some fronds from a cabbage palm and covered the body, and then he walked the road and gathered up some good-sized lime rocks for weight. It took four trips as he dropped them on top of the body until it sunk out of sight and pinning it to the bottom of the bog. Hunter checked the road at both ends for anyone traveling upon it. Satisfied that he was alone, he went to the horse that lay in the road. Hunter felt a sadness come over him for killing the horse. The man had it coming, but the animal was innocent. He wished he had the time to butcher the horse for meat, but doing this here in the open would be dangerous and there was no good place to cut here with swamp all around. Dragging the animal off the road was his only choice.

The Appaloosa was a good breed for riding, but Zeke did not take kindly to being used as a plow horse. It took Hunter's last two sugar cubes and some sweet talk, but soon Zeke was dragging the dead Mayer by rope along the side of the road. Hunter had the bowie knife ready as the carcass began to slide down the steep ditch; the short rope became taught and Hunter cut it, releasing Zeke from his burden. The heaviness of the horse rolled it down the bank and into the water, sinking only half-way. There were not enough rocks in the area to weigh the animal down, but he did cut more fronds in an attempt to cover it from the eyes of the buzzards.

The gunslinger mounted and took some water before lighting a smoke. He looked up to see the big black birds circling overhead. They had grown in number but there was nothing he could do about it. The gunslinger and Zeke headed back down the road with the dog following as two gators could be seen making their way down the canal toward the body of the horse. The meat would not go to waste after all, as the buzzards and the gators would soon be fighting over the carcass.

☐　☐　☐

Hunter decided to take a different route to Myakka City due to the fact that he was again a wanted man.

Traveling the road was no longer an option, so when he was able to leave the main route for back trails, he did just that. He took the smaller paths through the woods, which only slowed him down by an hour. He would come in across the cattle routes at the back of where Matt's Saloon stood. If it stood. If Myakka was up and running, there was a good chance that bounty hunters might be holed up there looking for information that would lead them to his whereabouts.

He stopped Zeke at the edge of the tree line and spied the city. Again, he missed his looking glass. He was behind Matt's Saloon at the edge of the woods. There was a large field where the crackers ran their cattle in-between him and the city's edge. There was smoke coming from the stack at the saloon, and he could see the third floor of the hotel towering behind; it had not been there long, for the wood on the building was new.

The sun was too high to cross the field without being seen, and Hunter had no idea who was running the town. He had decided he would wait until dark and then sneak in on foot. This would be the safest way to see if there were any friendlies about.

The war was over but there were still pockets of resistance, to be sure. The Union Red-legs were doing what they called "cleansing the country", and the Bushwhackers of the Confederacy had nothing left but to fight. Then there were men coming out of a war with no way to make a living but to hunt for bounty—and Hunter's bounty was set high.

Hunter dismounted and cleared a spot with his boot at the base of a pine tree. He looked and listened in all directions for any signs of intruders. Satisfied there was no one sneaking up from his back side, he sat and placed his hat over his eyes for a nap.

He didn't know how long he'd slept when he was awakened by a nudge at his shoulder. Hunter was surprised that it was the dog and not Zeke that was alerting him.

"What is it, girl? Is it time to eat already?"

The Lab took several steps back, turned and sat. She was facing the field, and beyond that was the town. Hunter followed her gaze to see someone had stepped out the back door of the saloon. He stood and watched closely.

"Well, I'll be...you old coot."

There was Walt dumping trash and throwing out the bath water. The distance was great, but there was no mistaking the old man's bent back and white whiskers that shone in the setting sun.

Hunter got to his feet and mounted his horse. He could not resist the look the dog was giving him, so he dug in the saddle bag and tossed a piece of jerky before they headed across the open field toward the back door of the saloon.

Walt had pitched the water and was wiping out the bowl when he glanced up and saw a rider and horse coming toward him from the woods. He reached for the butt of his revolver and then stopped, not believing what his eyes were seeing.

"Well, I'll be...you half-breed son-of-a-..."

There was no mistaking the painted horse and the long, straight black hair. Walt did not have to wait long to make sure he wasn't seeing things for the gunslinger had kicked Zeke into a canter and cleared the field quickly. Zeke whinnied with a hello which convinced Walt this was real and not some drunken dream.

"Howdy, you old coot."

"For a minute there, I thought I was lookin' at a ghost."

"The saddle soreness on my back-side tells me I am very much alive."

"Well, I'll be..." said Walt in disbelief. "You are one tough son-of-a-bitch!"

Hunter gave Walt a questioning look.

"Helen's good. She's about ready to pop. They've gone to the cabin, her and an Injun mid-wife and some braves. You would have crossed their path on the road, but you came in the back way. Smart."

Walt looked down at the dog. "I see you found a friend?"

"She found me; a chicken thief she is, but we worked it out."

The Lab looked from Walt to Hunter and back again, as if the dog knew they were talking about her.

"We claimed this town and built her back. Not all the news is good, Hunter: you're back on the wanted. We had a bounty hunter come through here with a poster lookin' for ya."

"Yep," replied Hunter. "I had a run in with a Texas Ranger a-ways back, but he won't be no more trouble."

"Well, that's good and bad," said Walt, "for the one that came through town weren't no Ranger, he's a known killer for hire."

"Where's this bounty hunter now?" Hunter asked.

"We run him outta town, but I doubt he went far."

Hunter dismounted and dug the last of the jerky from his saddle bag and threw a piece to the dog.

"The jerky and shine you left for me in the pit was a lifesaver Walt, but a steak and a beer sure would hit the spot."

"Come in through the back, Hunter James, and I'll git Amos to tend to Zeke." Walt disappeared through the back door. Hunter looked down at the Lab.

"Are you comin' with, dog?"

She sat and took a look at the saddle bag and then back to Hunter.

"Okay, you guard the jerky bag and I'll see you later."

Hunter dismounted and tied Zeke to an iron ring attached to the back of the building. He checked his guns, and then cautiously entered the back door of the saloon.

Chapter 11

The cattle town of Myakka was empty and silent. It would be a few weeks before the crackers came back through on their return cattle drive from the south, after delivering cattle to the keys for transport to Cuba. Their pockets would be full of money and their appetites for booze, women, and gambling would be vast, but until then, the Dolin Family would take that time to restock and then rest.

The gunslinger followed Walt across the street to the hotel where he greeted Jebidiah, Bodie, and Bird in the eating room. On the first floor, they ate steak and eggs prepared by Bessie. She almost dropped the plates as she entered and saw the gunslinger sitting at the big table. Hunter forced a smile toward her but as usual she put her head down and went about her work.

They discussed what had happened for the last six months while the gunslinger was gone. They all confessed that they presumed him dead; only Helen somehow knew he would survive. Hunter let them do the talking, not telling of his own experiences deep in the swamps; as white men, they would not have understood the powers of the medicine man and thought him crazy. Knowing the ancient ways of the Seminoles would just muddy the waters and it was easier for them to accept that he was alive only by God's will. Hunter believed in all of the above. He knew there was one Creator, but he figured white men and red men found God in different ways. Then, there were some that never found Him at all. Those men took another more evil path.

After his meal, Hunter stood and lit a fresh cigar given to him by Walt.

"Where can I bed down for the night? I'll be headin' to the cabin at first light."

"Third floor with a window over-lookin' the street. Bird will show you up."

Bodie looked over at Bird.

"Right away, for sure." Bird jumped up and waited for Hunter at the doorway.

"I want to thank y'all for watchin' over Helen. I'm in your debt," Hunter said. Then, he followed Bird out of the room and up the staircase.

☐ ☐ ☐

Hunter was at the barn before sunrise to find Zeke already saddled and ready for the trail. The brown Labrador was by the horse's side, protecting the saddle bag which had held the jerky. With a grin, the gunslinger tossed the dog a steak bone he had saved from last night's supper and watched with amazement as the bone was destroyed quickly with only a few crunching sounds.

Hunter checked over his gear, then adjusted the tension on the horse's belly strap. He heard the man outside before he entered and was at the ready, but eased as the middle-aged black man was unarmed.

"You do fine work. Me and Zeke, here, thank ya."

"Yes, sir. Is there anythin' else I's can do for ya?"

"All good." Hunter tossed the man a silver dollar. "What's your name?"

"Amos, sir. Thank ya, sir."

Hunter mounted as Amos opened the barn doors.

He rode out as the sun was just breaking through the trees. Zeke was rested and happy to be on the move as was the gunslinger. The dog followed as they broke into a canter.

It wasn't long before Hunter found trouble on a particular stretch of road that seemed to haunt him. He came across a rider-less horse grazing at the side of the road. It was saddled and loaded with gear except for an empty sheath where a rifle should be. Hunter quickly steered Zeke sharply off to the side and into the thicket just as a bullet nicked the brim of his hat followed by the loud crack of a rifle. The place where Hunter and Zeke had gone off the road was dry and the ridge wasn't too steep, but low enough to give cover.

Hunter slid from his saddle and pulled the paint to a tree lower into the ridge. He tied Zeke loosely and then looked for the dog. She was nowhere in sight. Hunter took his yellow boy rifle and made his way back up the ridge. He dropped to his belly and edged out to look down the road. He caught sight of the horse's tail disappearing into the woods on the other side of the thoroughfare about fifty yards to his left. Being shot at so early in the day angered Hunter, and he swore that he would not die here on this road after all he had been through.

Most men would hunker down and shoot from a distance or assess the situation before proceeding with caution, but not for this gunslinger on this day. Hunter slid down the bank and walked back to Zeke. He placed the rifle back in the saddle's sheath. He slid the double barrel sawed-off shotgun from his side shoulder holster and cocked back both hammers. He took a steady walk through the woods on his side of the road until he was across from where he saw the shooter's horse enter the thicket. When he reached the spot, he climbed the slope and crossed the thoroughfare, the two round holes of the ten gauges leading the way. His eyes were locked on that area with the awareness of a predator. From the edge of the road and looking down, he saw the horse between himself and the shooter, who was standing behind a southern pine. The gunman's rifle was aimed to the north, as he did not expect to be flanked.

Without breaking stride, Hunter pointed the shotgun straight up in the air and fired one barrel. The loud bang spooked the horse and set the animal into a run, clearing a shooting path to the gunman. The man turned, and Hunter could see the look of surprise on his face. They both fired at the same time. A bullet whizzed by Hunter's ear. The spray from the shotgun shattered bark from the southern pine and sent the gunman reeling backward. The rifle he held fell to the ground as the man rolled. He was wounded, but he came to his feet. One arm hung straight down, bleeding. With the other, he reached for the butt of his pistol. Hunter dropped the shotgun, still moving forward, and pulled his revolver while on the downhill side of the slope.

Only twenty feet away, Hunter's left palm came down hard and fast on the hammer of the Colt as he unloaded all six and aimed center mast; the gunman got off two shots wide right as he was slow. When the smoke cleared, the gunman lay on his back in a pool of his own blood that seeped from his chest. His neck was bent and his head was up, fighting to the last. Hunter had holstered the empty revolver and had pulled the other on pure instinct without thought. He put one shot in the man's forehead that snapped the head back, finally, to rest. The gunslinger was now standing over the body and reloading his weapons while he looked upon his kill. The shooter had a look of a mid-western man, not from these parts. Nothing that the man wore showed what side he had fought for in the war. North or South really didn't matter, for he had clearly been the enemy on this day.

Hunter went to one knee and rifled through the man's pockets; he found a cigarillo and a match, which he lit and puffed on while he continued. Hunter dug out two posters from inside the man's jacket and rolled them open. The first note read:

Wanted Dead for Murder
Half-Breed
Hunter James Dolin
5000 Dollars

The drawing forced a grin to Hunter's face, for the artist made him look more like an Indian than a white man. He slid the next poster out from under the first. It read:

Wanted Dead or Alive for Murder
Half-Negro Slave
Darnell
1000 Dollars

Hunter recognized the half-breed Negro man. He was a Florida boy, and had grown up a slave. The artist had drawn him more as a black man than a white man. Hunter began to see a pattern here and he also noticed that he was not given the option to be taken alive.

The guns the bounty hunter had carried were marked, so Hunter left them with the body. He took any ammo that he could use and relieved the dead

man of his money for he would not need it any longer. Hunter would not waste his sweat to bury a man
that would ambush another; in the gunslinger's eyes,
it was the coward's way.

He was done covering his tracks and decided to
leave the body where it lay in the woods and off the
road. This made him think of Helen, who would have
insisted that he give this man a Christian burial.
Helen wasn't here. Hunter collected Zeke and led him
by his reins up the slope and onto the road. He
mounted and looked around for the dog. After a moment, she appeared from out of the brush.

"There you are, girl. You ready to go home?"

Hunter was suddenly overcome by a feeling riding
on the wind as a breeze blew. *Helen was in trouble.*
He gave the horse a kick of his spurs. Zeke broke out
into a run down the thoroughfare. The dog followed,
struggling at first to keep up.

Hunter reached the area of the road where a clearing in the trees led to the shallow part of the river
fork. He turned hard and slowed the paint at the
water's edge. He could see the big oak and the cabin
that basked in its shade. Suddenly, three Indians
appeared on horseback from the side of the cabin
and two more with rifles were aiming at him from the
fence that surrounded the barn. Hunter reached into
his buckskin jacket and cocked both hammers back
on the shotgun, but left it in its holster as he moved
Zeke slowly forward. The two at the barn's corral had
a bead on him with the Winchesters, and at this
distance, they would not miss. While the three Indians on horseback rode hard toward him, he wrapped
the reins around the saddle horn to free up his
hands for the draw. Zeke felt Hunter's legs tighten on
his sides and his ears went back in alert, for the

veteran battle horse knew when he was steered in this manner that shots would soon follow.

As the Indians reached him, Hunter relaxed a bit for he recognized them as warriors of Sam Jones's band. *What are they doin' here?* It was true that this tribe had saved his life and the life of Helen, but Miccosukees were moody, and their superstitions drove them. One never knew when their minds might change; sometimes, as quickly as a drop of a hat.

The Seminole braves split apart and allowed Hunter to pass, but they never once took their eyes off him. Hunter took the reins and galloped the twenty yards to the front of the cabin, then slid down from the saddle. He glanced toward the barn to see the other two Indians had lowered their rifles and were mounting their horses pulled from the barn. Hunter surveyed the land about the farm looking for the Labrador who was nowhere to be seen. This was good, for you never knew how Indians might treat a dog. If threatened, they would not think twice about shooting an arrow through such an animal.

Hunter stepped onto the porch and when his hand touched the door handle, he suddenly froze when a strange sound came from inside; fear ran through the gunslinger. He could not remember being this scared since he was a boy. The sound he was hearing was that of a crying baby. He had to force himself to enter and as his eyes adjusted to the indoor light he saw Helen lying in a bed and an Indian woman standing by her side.

Tears ran down Helen's face when she saw him. He quickly went to her, leaning down and embracing her.

"I knew you were alive! I knew it all along in my heart," she muttered.

The baby cried out, which spooked the gunslinger. The portly middle-aged Seminole Indian woman came around to him. Hunter straightened up and took a step back. The Indian woman extended her arms to hand him the baby, but he just stood there and stared at it.

"Would you like to hold your son?" Helen asked while wiping the tears from her cheeks and smiling.

Hunter wiped his hands on his pants, stalling as much as cleansing, while he built up his courage. The Seminole woman made a face and extended her arms up, forcing him to take the baby which was wrapped in a bulky cloth. Hunter's eyes were unusually wide, and Helen laughed out loud.

"I don't want to break him," Hunter said in a serious voice. Helen laughed some more and the Seminole woman just scoffed at him.

"What's his name?" Hunter asked with an expression of amazement.

"James Mathew Dolin," said Helen, "if you agree."

Hunter mouthed his son's name followed by a rare grin.

"I reckon that would be just fine."

The new father stared at his son and all seemed good in the world until the baby suddenly began to cry. Hunter began to panic but was saved by the Indian woman who took the child and brought him to his mother.

"Baby's hungry," Helen said, as she sat up and removed the blanket that covered her top. Hunter leaned in and kissed her on the forehead.

"I got to take care of Zeke." He headed for the door. "I'll be right outside."

Hunter exited the cabin and stood on the porch breathing heavy as he pulled a cigar from his top pocket and lit it with a match struck from the back side of his britches. He inhaled deeply as a bead of sweat ran down his brow.

That was worse than any gunfight, Hunter thought, and then laughed at himself. He went to Zeke and patted him on the neck.

"Hats off to ya, Zeke. You're an uncle."

He shuffled through his saddle bag and found a bottle of whiskey as his supplies had been restocked by Amos. He pulled the cork and took a big swig, then watched the Miccosukee warriors cross the river in their departure. Hunter lifted his bottle in their honor and took another sip.

The Miccosukee warriors had protected Lus-tee Manito Nak-nee's woman while he was in the good hands of the Yaholi deep in the swamps. The half-breed's life was spared by the Great Spirit who was revered by the Seminoles, so they would keep their distance and return to their home.

Hunter looked down to see the dog had returned. He shuffled his hand in the saddle bag. The noise brought the dog in closer and to a sitting position in wait for a treat. Hunter tossed several chunks of jerked meat to the brown Lab and then he ate some himself.

The front door opened and Helen was being led by the Indian woman. Hunter quickly grabbed a wood rocker and slid it down the porch.

"Shouldn't you be in bed, '*mother*'?" asked Hunter.

"I've been in that bed for two days; it's time to git movin' around."

"Are you sure?" Hunter grabbed her arm and helped her to sit. The Indian woman had her arms crossed and was giving Hunter a look.

"It's not like I had been shot or am with sickness,

I've just given birth, is all."

"I think being shot would be easier," Hunter replied.

Helen introduced the Seminole woman. "This is Alameda, and I think her name means 'beautiful'."

"Really?" said Hunter with surprise, looking more shocked than he had meant too.

Helen now gave Hunter a scolding look. "She is a mid-wife sent by Sam Jones to help. I'd like to think the chief did it as an apology for the way he had treated me when we had first met, but I know that he sent her because he fears the spirits that run within you."

"Well, thank you for your help, Alameda," Hunter said, trying to sound sincere.

The Indian woman gave him a look that would stop a charging buffalo in its tracks. She then went inside the cabin and slammed the door behind her.

"She's not armed, is she?" Hunter asked with a look of his own.

"She may be here for a while, so you two need to try and git along."

"I will be sure to keep my distance," Hunter replied as he kissed Helen on the lips. At that moment, the dog appeared and went to Helen; she jumped up and placed her paws on the arm of the chair and licked Helen's face.

"Hey, dog!" said Hunter as he backed away and the dog muscled her way in.

Helen laughed with joy as she rubbed the dog's head and kissed her snout.

"And who is this pretty girl?"

"She's a chicken thief and a mooch. I would-a shook her off my trail long ago, but Zeke seems to like her around."

"Zeke, huh?" asked Helen. "What's her name?"

"*Dog* is as far as we've gotten."

"Well, that will not do." Helen held the dogs face in-between her hands as she spoke in a loving voice.

"I think you're the color of chocolate. That's it girl, your name is Mocha 'cause you're so sweet."

The dog licked Helen's face again as if she approved of her new name.

"I'll leave you two alone," said Hunter. "Zeke needs a good brush down, some water, and grain."

Hunter grabbed the reins and led the paint toward the barn. He looked back at Helen and a small grin appeared on his face before he could catch himself. *You're grinnin' an awful lot lately,* he thought, *like some babblin' fool.*

He was home with the woman he loved, a new baby boy and a good dog. He now had the family that he had always wanted, but that serene feeling left him quickly. His past always had a way of finding him. He knew that sooner or later, trouble would come.

Chapter 12

The morning came with the sun, and the humidity along with it. It was hot, and Hunter woke with a sweat. Helen and Alameda were already up and moving about the cabin preparing food. Hunter could not remember the last time he had slept so soundly and completely through the night. Mocha came to his bed side and licked his face, startling him for a moment.

"What are you doin' in here, dog?"

"I let her in," replied Helen as she stoked the fire in the wood stove. "She's family now."

"We'll have to set her a place at the supper table then," Hunter said with an eye roll as he sat up and slid his feet into his boots. He dressed and buckled on his weapons belt and then checked each gun for loads and jams. The guns needed a good break down and cleaning.

A cry rang out that suddenly reminded him he was a father. The sound made the cabin seem smaller and confined. He forced himself to walk over to the hammock that hung from the rafters and peered in on the baby. He was so small and helpless. For a moment, Hunter could feel something stirring in his heart. Suddenly, little James began to cry, and Alameda pushed Hunter out of the way to scoop up the baby. She scoffed at Hunter as she walked the child over to Helen. The Indian woman then left the cabin and slammed the door behind her.

"What in the heck was that all about?" Hunter

asked Helen as he crossed the room and kissed her on the forehead.

"She misses her family, I imagine. Being a midwife for a white woman must feel like punishment."

"Punishment for who?" Hunter asked. "She was sent here 'cause they fear my black heart and the spirits that dwell there."

"Your heart is good, gunslinger." Helen held James in one hand and with the other she palmed Hunter's face. "You are, at times, forced to fight bad men and some men can only be defeated by darkness."

"I don't know about all that, but I do what I have to do to survive."

Hunter put up his hand to stop her from replying as he cocked his head.

"Someone is comin'."

Alameda opened the front door and entered; she stepped aside allowing Hunter to leave the cabin. Mocha followed the gunslinger as she, too, felt a presence.

Hunter relaxed as he saw Bodie and Bird crossing the shallow creek at the fork of the river. They were moving with purpose but not with an urgency that warranted immediate action. He waited for them on the porch and Helen brought him a tin of coffee. She was wearing her guns around her waist that barely showed a bulge left over from the pregnancy.

"Ma'am," said Bodie with a tip of his hat.

Helen made a face at him.

"Sorry, ma'am—I mean, Helen."

"Jebidiah and Walt, they're good?" asked the gunslinger.

"They're good, holdin' down the fort for now, but two men rode in late last night flashin' around wanted posters."

"Let me guess, bounty hunters with posters that had half-breed written upon 'em?"

"Yup," replied Bodie, "we told them you were long dead to infection, last heard."

"But they didn't believe ya, did they, Bode?"

"No, sir, they did not, as far as I could tell. Bounty hunters are a suspicious lot and five thousand dollars keeps them very driven."

"Where are they now?" Hunter asked.

Bodie looked to Bird who answered the gunslinger, "I checked them into the hotel. I tried to put them in back but they were insistent, wantin' rooms at the front."

"Where the windows face the street?" Hunter added. "I'll take care of it. Bodie, I want you and Bird to do a little huntin' on the way back to town and don't show up without a kill; let them see."

"So them bounty hunters don't think we warned ya, that we just went on a hunt?" asked Bird.

Hunter nodded.

"You watch your ass, gunslinger," Bodie warned. "I know killers when I see 'em, and these boys are seriously that."

Bodie and Bird began to turn their horses, but were stopped by Hunter with one more question.

"You said they had posters?"

"The other one was of Darnell the cotton picker. He killed his owner right after he was freed, first chance he got. I don't recall the slave owner's name, but he was local."

Hunter nodded his head in acknowledgement, as he also recalled who they were.

"Git them bounty hunters drinking," continued Hunter. "Let 'em win at cards, whatever it takes to keep them up as long through the night as you can.

Tell Walt to give them the good whiskey. I want their heads hurtin' in the mornin' for I'll be there first light tomorrow."

"You got it." Bodie and Bird tipped their hats to Helen, then turned and rode off back the way they came.

"I'm goin' with ya," Helen blurted out.

"You gave birth just a few days ago and the boy needs milk. You're not thinkin', little lady."

Helen sighed with defeat, for she knew he was right. "I just got you back, Hunter James; you best not catch a bullet. I can't go through all that mess again."

"I'm back now, and I'm not goin' anywhere. Just a little ride into town to protect you and the family."

"Well, today you are mine," Helen said with a smile. "We will eat and enjoy this day together."

"Alright," agreed Hunter, "you, me, and little James. Oh, yeah, and Alameda, of course?"

"You be nice, Hunter James."

"It ain't me; I git that same evil eye from the Negro woman, what's her name? Bessie?"

"It ain't you. Well, you best find a way to git along. They're both part of the Dolin Family now."

"Yeah, okay." Hunter headed toward the barn. "I'm gonna go take care of Zeke."

"See you in a bit, and we'll have some food." She blew him a kiss before entering the cabin.

□　□　□

The plates were cleared from after the morning meal and the wood table was now scattered with gun parts. Hunter tore down the .44's and cleaned the powder residue that had built up due to the firing. Oil was applied inside and out, restoring the metal to a shine. The revolvers were worn but well taken care of. If the guns could speak, they would have many tales of death to tell. Guns were merely tools of these times, and it was the men behind them that determined whether they were used for good or evil, for which there was a fine line. The Half-Breed Gunslinger's line was so fine, it was damn near invisible at times...when it came down to kill or be killed, his line would re-appear, and his justice would be done.

Hunter cleaned and oiled the sawed-off, double barrel ten gauged shotgun and his yellow boy, .45-Colt Winchester rifle until they shined and all levers moved freely. Afterward, he set out behind the barn and chose several trees at different distances for targets and emptied each model to its capacity, making sure all were in working order. Not one shot missed its mark.

The sun seemed to cross the sky slower today, for Hunter was itching to confront the business that awaited him. He did not enjoy killing but when one was hunted for a bounty, it was kill or be killed.

They ate supper that night early at Hunter's request, and Zeke was saddled and ready prior to the eating of the meal. Helen was not happy when she realized he would not sleep at the cabin this night but on the road. They sat together under the big oak by the river and talked. Both were reminded of the first time they had a conversation and spoke of a possible future.

Hunter tried to explain why he would sleep on the trail and away from her.

"You must understand, my lady; for a man like me, my energy is drawn from the land, the stars in the sky and from the winds that blow. I cannot explain why, only that it is. My senses are dulled when confined to the indoors."

"You do what you have to do, gunslinger, to git back to us in one piece. I'll wait here for you like I always have done. Now, you go on—before I change my mind."

Hunter mounted the paint and headed for the fork of the river stream that led to the road that usually brought trouble. He stopped at the stream's edge and looked back to see the brown dog on his trail.

"You stay, girl; this is your home now."

Mocha looked up at him and then she looked back at the cabin, and then back to Hunter and Zeke. Helen showed with a piece of fatty meat left over from supper and that was all it took to keep the Lab from following.

Hunter thought, as he moved on through the water to the other side, *That's why you're a survivor, dog. The loyalty to your stomach holds no bounds.*

Chapter 13

The gunslinger sat upon his horse just outside of the new Myakka City an hour before dusk and went through the ritual of checking his guns. He smoked and sipped water from his canteen and then took two good slugs from a whiskey bottle before riding slow into town.

He was alert and prepared for battle as his mind had been set that night as he had slept on a limestone hammock surrounded by the tall grasses under the star-filled skies of the Florida swamp. Two hours of sleep was all that was needed to sharpen his wits.

Zeke could sense the tension build as they got closer to town, for the painted horse had carried the gunslinger into many battles and he knew when the man was feeling anxious.

They stopped in the middle of the road not far from Matt's Saloon as the sunlight broke through the trees. Hunter threw his cigar butt to the ground. From under the brim of his hat, he saw two men come out of the saloon and stagger down the steps and into the street. They wore their guns set for killing by the draw, not just bounty hunters but gunfighters. Hunter dismounted noisily and dropped flat-footed to the ground intending to get their attention, but the long night of drinking had dulled their minds as Hunter had planned, and they did not notice him, at first.

Hunter removed his buckskin jacket and draped it over the saddle. He pulled one pistol and spun it forward, then backward. He spun the cylinder and then pulled back the hammer; the distinct sound caught the two men's attention as they had crossed the road and reached the foot of the hotel steps. They both turned and watched the gunslinger holster his weapon and begin to walk toward them. The gunfighters looked at one another, and without a word began to fan out, one on each side of the street.

Hunter could tell these two had worked together before by the way they moved into place, communicating only with a glance. He also noticed the whiskey stagger was gone now that the risk of death was assured. As professionals, they could sober up at will, but after a long night they might be a bit slower on the draw. Hunter was counting on it, for as good as he was, it was still two against one—and a gunfighter was always looking for an edge. The sun was at Hunter's back as he had planned, but the clouds were many and covering up any glare that he could use to his advantage.

Hunter stopped in the center of the street twenty-five paces from the gunfighters. The man on Hunter's left had walked back, just off the steps of the saloon, two .45's hung from his waist. The other man to Hunter's right stayed in front of the hotel; he had a single .45 in a short holster and what looked like a .32 was stuck in his belt.

There was no wind and the air was thick. The only sound on this quiet morning was the thump of the heartbeat in the inner ears of each man that stood tall in the face of death.

Seconds went by that seemed like minutes, and Hunter had a notion that these two may be having second thoughts about their situation. He figured he might give them a chance to drop those hammers and move on with their lives.

"I hear you boys been lookin' for me," stated Hunter; his eyes moved from one man to the other, constantly looking for movement.

"You be the half-breed wanted for murder on my poster? I'd say if you weren't that man then you wouldn't be here ready to draw, I reckon?" said the slightly older man on the left.

"Five thousand dollars dead," said the other man to Hunter's right. He was tall and thin with a long face, under a worn-out derby hat. "If you were to give up them guns right now, taking you alive may be an option—"

"You know, you two can just ride on," replied Hunter. "This doesn't have to be. There are plenty of wanted rebels in Missouri and Texas, I'll bet."

"We're not in Texas, half-breed, and the Red-legs got Missouri covered pretty well. I didn't ride all the way down her in this skeeter-infested swamp to turn back empty-handed," the older man said with teeth clenched.

The derby wearer on Hunter's right made his move. He drew the .45 with impressive speed, but to his bad luck, Hunter's eyes had moved on him just before he drew and the Half-Breed Gunslinger was a tick faster. Hunter's single .44 shot went through the man's stomach. The return fire whizzed between Hunter's chest and under his armpit, tearing his shirt, the bullet only missing by a hair.

The elder gunfighter on Hunter's left had pulled his pistol a half-second after his partner, and fired with the aim of a professional. His bullet would have hit its mark if Hunter had not dropped to one knee with a turn and emptied the remaining five shots; his hand was a blur. His palm came down hard and fast on the hammer. The gunfighter shook violently backward with every shot, and landed hard on the front porch of the saloon with a thud. Hunter turned immediately back to the other man who amazingly had managed to get to his feet and was grabbing for the .32 in his belt.

Hunter was empty, and went for his other revolver, but to his surprise it was not there; the left side gunman's bullet had torn the holster enough to dump the weapon to the ground. Luckily for Hunter, the blood from the man's stomach, at his right, had run down and soaked the handle on the .32. It was slick to the point where he had a hard time getting a grip on it. This gave Hunter time to pull the shotgun from his side shoulder holster and cock both hammers back. The sound and sight stopped the derby hat wearing gunfighter in his tracks.

"You got three seconds to drop it."

The man had one hand over his wound and the other was holding the .32 halfway up, but not yet level. Hunter could see in his eyes that he was weighing his options. As soon as Hunter saw his arm that held the .32 flinch, Hunter pulled both triggers that blew the man backward, throwing him onto the porch of the hotel far enough that his head hit the swinging bat doors, leaving the body motionless over the threshold.

The silence was deafening and the street was filled with smoke as all this had taken only minutes. Hunter quickly glanced around for anyone that might take a shot at him in his vulnerable state, for his weapons were empty. He walked over and picked up his fallen revolver and checked to see that it did still function.

Hunter was sweating and breathing heavy as he reloaded his weapons. Walt stepped around the dead man that lay motionless on the saloon's porch and made his way to the gunslinger's side with a bottle in his hand.

"Here you go, son." Walt handed him the whiskey. "You sure as hell got nine lives, there, gunslinger, and I'll be damned if I don't git a kick every time you pull them pistols."

"I don't enjoy killin', Walt," Hunter replied calmly as he took a swig.

"Well, that's a shame son, 'cause you're damn good at it and a man should enjoy what he's good at."

Hunter turned toward the road and blew out a sharp whistle. Zeke came straight away to his side with a trot. Hunter took the reins and gave the horse a pat on the neck.

The few people that worked the town had appeared from around every corner. Hunter noticed Bessie was staring down at the body on the steps from the doorway of the saloon. She glanced up at him with a look of disdain that he had seen from her many times before. Bessie then shot back inside, leaving the swinging doors to settle on their own.

Jebidiah had joined Walt and Hunter in the street.

"Well, there be two more unmarked graves for the boneyard," Jebidiah said as he rubbed his chin whiskers. "You had no choice, son. They weren't gonna give it up."

"They never do, Jeb."

Bodie and Bird had collected the dead men's guns and had joined the rest.

"Can't hardly blame 'em," said Bird. "Five thousand dollars is a lotta money." When he said this, he got a look from Walt and Jebidiah.

"What? Jeez, you old coots, I'm just sayin'."

"Bird."

"Yeah, Bode?"

"Git Amos and fetch the wagon; let's git them bodies off the street. The crackers could be ridin' through here any day now and it's gonna git busy around here with a whole new set of troubles."

Bird walked away and met Amos at the hotel steps.

"Two more bodies for the boneyard, Amos," Bird yelled with excitement as they ran off to fetch the wagon.

The plot of land where the bodies were buried was almost the size of the town itself. Some of the graves were unmarked to discourage any kin from seeking revenge. The marked ones were a reminder to all that justice was done.

□   □   □

Hunter, Walt and Jebidiah ate their morning meal in the saloon, washed down with whiskey spiked coffee. Hunter told them of the new addition to the Dolin Family, a boy named after his father—and that Helen and James Mathew Dolin were doing well.

"That would make us grand pappies, Walt," Jebidiah said with a chuckle.

"Dang, Jeb, that finally proves it; I'm gittin' too old for this shit." Walt dumped more whiskey in his coffee cup. He drank half of it, and then filled it again.

Jebidiah took advantage of Walt's thirst to get a word in.

"I had been meanin' to talk at ya, son, about them

wanted posters that keep turnin' up in the hands of them bounty hunters."

Jebidiah paused for a moment, waiting for Hunter to reply. When he didn't, Jebidiah continued.

"They're gonna keep comin' until that bounty's lifted off your head, I figure."

There was a pause as Hunter sipped his whiskey-laden coffee. He glanced at Jebidiah and then toward Walt from under the brim of his hat.

"Alright, Jeb, spit it out," said Hunter as he slipped a smoke from his top pocket. "Who's put the money on my head?"

"It's a woman; goes by the name of Jane."

"And tell me, Jeb, what might this *Jane's* full name be?"

"It's ah...Montgomery, Jane Montgomery."

"Well, that's a problem, ain't it?" said the gunslinger. "If it was a Montgomery brother, an uncle or even a young boy, well that's one thing; but a woman...can't kill a woman."

"Yep," replied Walt, "that would be a dilemmer."

"Well, there may be a way," said Jebidiah.

"What are you talkin' about, Jeb? Killin' a woman is a hangin' offense, not to mention it just ain't right." Walt was suddenly serious.

"Hold on, there. Hear me out. I been thinkin' on this: a man can't kill a woman, but a *woman* could kill a woman."

"No," Hunter replied sternly. "Ain't no way in hell."

"You crazy, Jeb?" said Walt. "You talkin' 'bout Helen, ain't ya?"

"I know I know, but she's good with them guns. Alright, you're right; forgets I mentioned it. It was just a thought."

Hunter stood and looked from one old man to the

other.

"Don't neither one of you mention this to Helen, you hear me? You just put that thought right out of your whiskey-soaked heads."

Walt and Jebidiah agreed as Hunter took his smoke with him out the doors and onto the front porch. He stopped and smeared the blood that lay on the wood with the bottom of his boot; he then jerked his head up as Bird yelled out. "Yaw!"

Bird and the black man steered the wagon toward the edge of town with two tarp covered mounds in the back. The sounds of the wood wheels and the horses' rig rattled as they rode off. The last sound that stuck in the gunslinger's mind was the distinct clanking of the metal shovels bouncing off one another. They were headed for the boneyard, the bounty hunters' final resting place—and their last stop above ground.

Chapter 14

Hunter had returned to the Dolin cabin, and so far, he had spent several weeks at home with Helen, little James, and Alameda. He tried his best to gain favor with the Indian woman. She had attacked him twice with a broom, reminding the gunslinger that the women were really running the farm. He was thankful that none of the boys were around to witness his humiliation, but in the end, Hunter figured it was worth the beatings to see Helen beam with smiles of laughter and to watch the dog defend him from the sweeper. They had all gained the dog's trust and the brown Labrador was now part of the family. She had accepted Mocha as her name and would even sit for a bath, but only for Helen.

Hunter had cut a square hole in the bottom of the cabin's front door with a leather flap so the dog could come and go as she pleased. Mocha slept the nights in the cabin and she would always lie down directly under the baby's hanging crib as if on guard. Little James was growing like a weed, and with Alameda working with the boy, he would be crawling and walking in no time. The Indians did not pamper their children like the whites did; they put them to the test early in life. In the wild, their skills and strength were what they would need for their survival.

Hunter and Mocha had left the cabin in the fourth week to replenish their food supply. They did not have to travel far, for this area was rich with wild game. A day's ride into the swamp, another day's ride back and two days for the hunt was all it took to stock up on some meat.

Near the end of the first day out, Hunter ran across tracks of a large buck, and with help from Mocha, they had run him down. With a precise shot from the Winchester, the buck ran no more.

The barn was used for salting and hanging of the meat, and parts were sliced and put in the dry boxes for jerky over a slow fire. Bones and hide had their purposes and not one piece would go to waste.

The second four-day run bagged two gators, one five-footer and another slightly bigger. Mocha surrounded the reptile and ran around barking and growling in the shallow waters, keeping it busy. With a quick step from the hindmost, the full thirteen inches of Hunter's bowie knife was thrust through the brain just behind the eyes. This was the best method of putting down the beast. Too many times, Hunter had seen a gator come back to life after being shot even several times, to find it was only temporarily lifeless.

Hunter built a sled to drag the gators back to the cabin for the bulk and weight was too much for Zeke's back to bear, and this would allow Hunter to ride instead of walk. On the trail, they stopped for lunch and ate Mocha's favorite meal of fire spit chicken. There was an abundance of wild guineas, also known as the spotted fowl, running around this area. Watching the dog devour the chicken meat reminded Hunter of someone, and he asked the dog questions on the matter.

"Stumpy, are you in there?" he asked while staring into the dog's eyes.

"If I didn't know better, dog, I'd say you might

have been a chicken eatin' midget once in another life, huh, girl?"

Mocha turned her head in a comical way which got a smile from the gunslinger, as he tossed her another piece of chicken meat.

"I'd bet my bottom dollar that if I had some acorn beer you'd lap it right up."

Hunter wished Jeb and Walt were here, for they would get the joke. They knew the little midget man that once guarded the bridge from years past. The half-man had choked on a turkey leg bone that Hunter had given him for payment of passage across the river's bridge. Hunter supposed the turkey's spirit had gotten his revenge.

On the way back to the cabin with the gator carcasses, there was a period of time that put the gunslinger on edge, for he had the sense that they were being followed. Mocha sensed a presence, and several times, she dropped back behind the sled and growled at something that clearly smelled of wet, skunky fur. Hunter picked up the pace, and soon they were on the stretch of road that led to home. He knew of the beast that had been following them. The gunslinger feared no man, but the creature that stalked the swamps always left him with a feeling of dread.

Hunter skinned the gators and secured the meat, once at the homestead. He took both gator heads and found a large collection of ant piles at the north end of the property. The fire ants would clean the heads down to the bone. The gator skulls would look impressive hanging on the front of the cabin for all to see. Alameda would finally have to acknowledge his great skills as a hunter like that of her people. The Indian woman stopped and looked as he walked by with the gator skulls. She then looked at Hunter without any expression, and walked away with an empty basket toward the garden.

Hunter glanced at Helen with disbelief.

"Well, at the least she didn't scoff at you; that's somethin'," assured Helen. "Maybe she don't care for gator meat?"

"Well, we're going out again tomorrow. Maybe a little pig will cheer her up?"

□ □ □

The last run of their hunt turned out to be the most dangerous. The risk of hunting deer was minimal; the killing of gators was very dangerous, and many wranglers had lost limbs, but one of the most treacherous beasts in the swamp was the wild boar. They thrived in the swamps and grew very large with tusks that could gut a horse with one charge. The four hundred-pound hog that Hunter and Mocha cornered was not going down without a fight. Zeke did not spook easily, but when it came to these large pigs, he could not help showing fear. The horse broke loose as he began to panic. Zeke ran off through the thicket as Mocha barked and growled, circling and corralling the boar.

"Dammit, horse!" muttered Hunter. He had not removed his rifle before the Appaloosa had cut through the brush in search of the safety of the trail. The gunslinger would have to fight the beast up close and personal, and he would have to end its life quickly. Mocha was a good size for a Labrador, but she looked like a pup next to the large boar. The hog charged her and just missed her belly as Mocha jumped back with a turn. Hunter decided he must set a charge of his own before his dog ended up hanging from the pig's eight-inch tusks.

Moving forward, the gunslinger pulled both .44's and pulled the hammers back with his thumbs. He pulled the triggers in a slow, melodic way like that of a musician. Smoke followed the booms of the .44's. Four shots had been fired and two slugs had gone through the shoulder as the hog was whipping around in a dance with the dog. The boar circled around a large pine tree that blocked four more of Hunter's shots. The bark flew, and Hunter cussed at the surprise of his inaccuracy. For such a large target, the hog was surprisingly swift.

He emptied the revolvers with the last two shots that hit the beast in the side and hind quarters, which seemed to anger it further. The boar left the dog and began a charge; it was a short distance. Hunter dropped his revolvers to the ground and pulled the shotgun that hung on his side. He pulled the hammers back, and from the hip, he aimed for the head as it came forward. As soon as he pulled the triggers, Hunter cringed, for Mocha had jumped up on the back of the pig and possibly in the line of fire. At the last second, Hunter brought the barrels down as the shotgun boomed, knocking him a couple of steps back and putting the hog, snout first, into the ground right at the gunslinger's feet and close enough to splatter blood on his pant legs and boots. The wild boar was dead, but as Hunter feared, he heard a yelp and saw Mocha fall and disappear behind the pig's large body.

He dropped the shotgun and ran around the carcass in a panic. He grabbed his dog and cradled her as she opened her eyes and licked his face. Hunter dug through the fur where there was blood. He exhaled with a sigh of relief, for she had only caught a few lead pellets in the shoulder, as he could see their dull shine. Hunter could easily remove them, for they did not get too deep.

"You're alright, girl. I can dig those out without much fuss."

Mocha wiggled from his arms and ran around him wagging her tail. Then, she moved around to the front of the boar and began barking and growling. The hair on the back of her neck stood straight up.

"It's dead, girl. You did good, you're a hell of a warrior."

Mocha stopped barking and began to sniff around the body. She growled slightly and low, and then her tail began to wag again.

"Now let's find that cowardly horse."

Mocha barked at him in a response as if she were defending Zeke's honor. They walked up the trail with their heads held high. It had been a great battle and they were feeling good to be alive.

☐ ☐ ☐

The barn was loaded down with different kinds of the hanging, salted meats from several weeks of the hunt. Dry boxes smoked for days with the hanging slivers of jerky that was then packed in leather bags for travel on the road. Alameda grew onions, corn, tomatoes and different kinds of greens in a small garden. There were chickens for eggs, and a goat for milk. The cabin was shaded by the large oak and the big river flowed on one side, the small creek running on the other, giving fresh water. Mullet swam upstream from the oceans along with blue crab the size of Hunter's spread hand. Fresh and salt water fish, manatees and gators, all shared the waters with gars and bluegill. The cabin was a perfect home for anyone.

Hunter James Dolin looked around the small farm. No matter how hard he tried, he could not feel at ease here. He had a sense of danger, always. He was a wanted man, and he would never be at peace until all bounties were lifted.

Hunter felt an urgency to get Helen back up to par with her target shooting. It had been the gunslinger's experience that idle weapons lost their accuracy. He set up bottles and tin cans along the back fence posts behind the cabin. He then fired three shots from his Colt into the air at a rapid pace, and then he counted the seconds in his head, *one Okeechobee, two Okeechobee, three Okeechobee, four Okeechobee, Five...*

Helen appeared, running from the house toward him with her pistols pulled and cocked. He saw the Indian woman running from her garden to the house to tend to the little one.

"Just under five seconds; a little slow, my lady."

Breathing hard, Helen looked at Hunter and then to the targets and then back to him. "Really? You made me run out here to shoot at targets? I got a three-month-old in there that, thanks to Alameda, is already crawling around and gettin' into things. You scared the heck outta me!"

"Good, we need to be a little scared; I fear we're gittin' a little soft out here. When you git soft, you let down your guard; letting down your guard adds up to a dirt nap."

"What are you talkin' about, Hunter? Can't you just relax and enjoy what God has blessed us with? For cryin' out loud."

"The Lord gives it and the Lord takes it away... well, it's the takin' away part that I'd like to be ready for."

"You, of all people, quoting Bible verses?" Helen slid her Dragoons back into their holsters and then began to walk away. "There's hope for you yet, gunslinger."

"Helen, please—you need to take what I'm sayin' serious."

Helen stopped her departure and walked up close to him. "Tell me what's goin' on and I'll listen; there's somethin' you're not tellin' me."

Hunter took a deep breath in thought, and then exhaled strong with the sound of defeat. He pulled a rolled paper from his inside jacket pocket and handed it to her. Her eyes did not leave his as she unrolled it. She then looked at it and began her study.

"Where did you git this?"

"I ran into a bounty hunter on the road; he carried it on his person."

"What happened?" she asked in a tone that said she really didn't want to hear.

"Let's just say he won't be a bother any longer."

She still had the poster rolled open in her hand. She studied it further.

"The drawin' don't even look like you," Helen said, irritated.

"That don't matter much. How many Half-Breed Gunslingers are runnin' around these parts? Now, no more questions; can we please knock some dust off those Dragoons?"

Helen handed him back his paper and, with respectable speed, she drew one pistol and with a turn she slammed the hammer down five times, fanning out and shattering three bottles and a tin can. The can flew straight up in a spin. She holstered the empty pistol and pulled the left one. She fired once, hitting the can out of the air. It spun some more and then dropped to the ground.

"You missed one," said Hunter; the tone of his voice was that of a teacher scolding a pupil.

Helen holstered her gun and stomped over to the can that lay on the ground. Hunter couldn't help but grin, as he knew she was irritated. He watched her from behind. Her hips swung in a shake that would put most men to one knee, flowers in hand.

Helen picked up the can. She examined it and then walked back to him. Hunter now watched her from the front; her movements were amazing, and it took some discipline for him not to sweep her off her feet and take her into his arms. The thoughts running through his mind were not even close to what was on hers.

Not saying a word, Helen shoved the can into his hand with a grin and walked off toward the house. She reloaded the five shot pistols as she walked away.

Hunter looked at the can to see it had three bullet holes in it which accounted for all six shots, one for each of the three bottles and two must have hit the can. The sixth shot was from the second draw as the can spun in the air.

The gunslinger was about to call out to Helen when he suddenly felt he was being watched. He turned his head quickly and looked to a thick tree line across the main river. The trees blew in a steady breeze as he panned with his eyes for any movement out of the normal. Mocha approached him from the rear. The dog came alongside of him and sat staring at the same tree line across the river.

"There's someone out there, ain't there girl?"

Mocha woofed once as she sensed the danger that the gunslinger felt. Hunter wished he had the spy glass and made a mental note to purchase a new one. The wind continued to blow and the feeling of a presence had gone. The dog was the first to lose interest and she went about sniffing and marking her territory.

Sam Jones made a habit of keeping an eye on the white men who lived and hunted the Seminole lands. He did this for good reason. Hunter figured if the chief had sent the Miccosukee, they would have allowed themselves to be known to him. No, someone else had been watching them...

Helen met up with Hunter in the barn where he was working on the rigging of Zeke's saddle. Mocha was by her side, and Hunter had a suspicion that the dog had alerted her to his movements. He gave Mocha a look and she ducked in behind Helen. Mocha then poked her head out from around the back of Helen's legs.

"I know you are at your best from the back of a horse, Hunter James, but I need to know your plans so I can do my part."

Hunter avoided Helen's eye contact as he adjusted the horse's belly strap several times, searching for the right tightness. She waited patiently for him to speak.

"The tobacco and whiskey supplies are getting low. With the crackers comin' through town soon, there may be some new information from the north."

Helen rubbed Zeke's neck as she walked around the horse to the other side to face him. Their eyes met.

"You trained me to be a gunslinger and my place is by your side."

"Your place is to take care of the little one," he flatly stated.

She made a face as she was not sure how to argue that.

"You just bring your butt back here in one piece, mister," she demanded.

"I always do," he said with a grin.

Helen was smiling on the outside, but she was worried on the inside. This was the way it had to be, for now.

"When the boy is off the teat, I will be fightin' by your side until this craziness is over. No matter how many we have to kill to protect what we've built here, for our family...for our son. Promise me," Helen stressed.

He did not say it but he did nod in agreement. She went to her toes and kissed him on the lips. The dog barked twice as the gunslinger mounted up. Without further words, he rode off through the opened barn doors and headed for the stream past the big oak. The dog continued barking as he spurred Zeke into a canter. Mocha stayed behind, knowing this was her home and her job was to protect Helen and the baby.

Hunter managed his troubled stretch of road without incident, and worked his way around to the other side of the river where he and Mocha suspected a watcher had set. He dismounted and checked his weapons. He then tied Zeke loosely to a scrub oak and entered the woods on foot. Right off, he spotted shod hoof prints in the sand. The Indians did not ride shod ponies unless they were stolen from the white man, and there were only one set of tracks.

The Seminoles rode in groups, so this could only mean one thing: the watcher who set up here was a *gringo*. Hunter followed the trail to what was the spot of observation behind a large cluster of Spanish moss-covered cypress trees just outside the river's edge. He looked across the water to see the back of the cabin and the fence where they had stood for the shooting of the targets. Hunter went to one knee and pulled a snuffed-out cigar butt from the dirt. *A cigar smoker; well, that certainly narrows it down,* Hunter thought with much sarcasm.

On his way back to Zeke, Hunter noticed something peculiar about one of the hoof prints: there was a lightning bolt-shaped chip from what looked like the left front hoof. This was proof he could use to identify the rider's horse. Then again, most bounty hunters where partial to ambush, and he may never see the man that might collect the bounty on him.

Hunter moved out toward town with gambling on his mind. He hoped he could catch the crackers passing through and relieve them of some of their money. He was eager to drink whiskey with the boys, surrounded by the smells of a saloon and the sounds of shuffling cards and clinking coins filling the smoky air. If he never heard another baby crying in his lifetime, it would be too soon.

Chapter 15

The cow town of Myakka had finally settled down after two weeks of revelry. The cracker cowboys had passed through on their way back north with pouches full of wages from their cattle drives to the south. The trouble they caused was no worse than usual, but trouble there was, and plenty of it.

Bodie did not wear a badge, but the role he played in these booming periods of time was that of a town sheriff. Bird, Jebidiah and Walt acted as deputies. It was their town and they made that clear to anyone who entered. The sign said Myakka City, but at its best, a cattle town was all it would ever be.

This morning, all four men sat at tables in the saloon as Bessie served them coffee, fried mullet and grits with fried potatoes. Walt drank beer, and there was a bottle of whiskey at the table setting, but no one dared it just yet. They had risen this morning with the first good night's rest in weeks and they cherished the quiet as they discussed the goings on of future town business.

"I'm gittin' too old for this shit." Walt stood up and held out his beer to begin the meeting.

"You say that every time, you old coot," Bird replied, which sent chuckles around the table.

"You'll be sayin' the same when you're at my age, you baby whipper snapper," spouted Walt. "Now pass me that bottle before I put a boot in your ass."

"Alright you two, must we start every meetin' this

way?" Jebidiah complained as he swirled a piece of pan fried river mullet around in his grits before he brought it up for a bite.

Bird continued with his banter, ignoring Jebidiah. "Think on all the money we're makin' there, old man. This was the best haul yet, I reckon?"

"What good's money, boy, if I'm pushin' worms six foot under?" Walt asked, followed by a belch.

Bird began to spout back when he caught a look from Bodie that stopped him. He filled his mouth with a spoonful of taters as if to force the words back.

Jebidiah took this moment to break in before they started up again.

"Yep, it was a good haul, but what we need to talk on is a growing problem."

"Which problem would that be, Jeb?" Bodie asked.

"It's what I overheard the other night at that poker table right over there." Jebidiah pointed to the south corner of the saloon. "Two of them crackers; I ain't sure who they rode for, but they were talkin' 'bout the five thousand dollars on the head of Hunter James Dolin."

"That ain't good," said Bodie. "Bounty hunters is bad enough, but now we got local cow hands lookin' to cash in. The only way I see to stop this is to git the money off the table."

"The only way to do that is to kill that Montgomery woman," said Walt, "and that is a hangin' offense."

"Not if another woman does it..." Jebidiah replied. As soon as he said this, a voice from behind him made him twitch.

"I thought we agreed not to speak on that subject?" said Hunter as he entered through the swinging doors.

"Jesus all mighty, gunslinger," said Jebidiah with his hands on his chest. "You give an old man a heart attack."

Hunter pulled a chair and sat at the table. He removed his hat and used his fingers to draw back his long black hair.

"I still don't git how you can walk those wood steps in them boots and make no sound," Bodie said as he released the hammer on his revolver. He hadn't had the time to draw his pistol, but his hand did make it to the butt, and his thumb to the hammer.

"It's that Indian blood runnin' halfway through him. I had seen them sneaky Injuns in the Seminole Indian wars, quiet as a mouse they were..."

"Walt," Jebidiah said sternly.

"Hell, I don't mean no offense by it, just tellin' a dang story." Walt cheered the gunslinger with a tip of his cup.

Hunter took no offense from Walt's words—it was just his way. Bessie came in from the back and dropped a plate in front of the gunslinger and then she shot back without a word.

Jebidiah spoke direct as Hunter worked his plate. "I don't like the I-dear much, neither, son, but she's as good a shot as most men I've seen. If you don't want to spend the rest of your days lookin' back over your shoulder, it may be the only way."

"I need to think on it," said Hunter. "If there's another way, I want to find it."

"Fair enough, son, I git it," Jebidiah replied.

Bird didn't say much to anyone, and he talked even less when the gunslinger was about. He had ideas, but he feared ridicule and usually kept his thoughts to himself. He had smarts but struggled with confidence, and right now, he was building up his courage to speak, but he was suddenly cut off by Walt.

"Welp, we got work to do," Walt said as he stood, which sent others to their feet. "Them cowboys sure made a mess of this place and I would like to be done cleanin' up before nap time."

Bird stood up so fast his chair fell back and hit the floor. "You old coot!" he shouted as he stormed out of the saloon.

"What's got into his britches?" Walt directed his question toward Bodie.

"Youngsters, hell, I don't know. I'll set that energy of his to good use."

Bodie left the saloon and Jebidiah followed. Walt took to the upstairs to clean the rooms, leaving Hunter alone to eat his morning meal. The mullet was pan fried in corn meal to a crunchy perfection and he thought he tasted a bit of butter in the grits, which was a luxury for a man that spent most of his time on the trail.

Hunter went to the bar and poured himself a draft beer. He saw Bessie come in from the kitchen with a plate in her hands. She appeared to be heading for the stairs. Their eyes locked; he wasn't sure what to say or do, and she was waiting to see if he needed anything before she went to her room to eat. Before Hunter knew what he was saying, he blurted out something that surprised them both.

"Miss Bessie, will you please join me at the table?"

They stared at each other for a moment, and then they both moved to where Hunter's unfinished meal awaited. He stood until she sat and then he joined her. Across from each other, they ate in silence, only looking at one another occasionally. This went on for what seemed like forever for them both. They finished their meals at about the same time. Bessie stood, suddenly forcing Hunter to jump up while shoveling the last bite into his mouth. She took his plate and then reached out for his fork. He handed it over, and for some reason, he had stopped chewing. Bessie nodded to him and took away the dishes, leaving Hunter standing alone with a mouth full of grits.

He soon figured out she wasn't coming back and he relaxed. They had not spoken to one another, but Hunter felt they had made progress toward an understanding of each other. For the first time, she did not seem as scared of him as she had before, which pleased him. It also reminded him that he was more comfortable being shot at than dealing with the emotions of women. With Bessie and Alameda he did not stand a chance; but Helen, at least, understood him. In fear that Bessie might return, he grabbed a bottle of whiskey from the table and headed out for the comfort of his horse.

Zeke was glad to see him, especially when Hunter produced an apple from his saddle bag. He cut it in half with the Bowie knife, and with his palm bent upward he fed the horse one piece at a time, careful not to allow his fingers to get in the way.

Hunter watched around town as the hired hands cleaned up the streets. All the hitching posts had been full for weeks and there was a lot of manure to be shoveled. It wasn't a glamorous job, but a necessary one that paid real money for out-of-work slaves and local youngsters.

Hunter suddenly heard a door slam at the side of the saloon where Walt came out of a newly built shed. The stack that jutted through the roof told Hunter it was a still where the moonshine was brewed for the Okeechobee, and the making of the apple pie. Supply wagons ran through town regularly delivering Kentucky bourbon and brewed chuck beer, but between bad weather and robberies there were times when Walt's swills saved the day.

A window opened on the second floor of the saloon and Jebidiah slung dirty water from a wood bucket down to the street. Jebidiah spotted Hunter and gave him a nod; Hunter returned it, and then Jebidiah stuck his head back inside and was gone.

Bodie and Bird were inside the hotel cleaning and preparing for the next wave of cow hands that would pass through here in a month or two. Hammers were hard at work on the outside of the hotel as two Cuban carpenters replaced a broken window on the first floor. Hunter suddenly realized he was not needed here unless there was killing to be done. He decided then that he should be at the cabin with Helen. In his gut, he knew sooner or later that his skills would be needed as trouble would surely find him—as it always did.

Before Hunter mounted up and headed home, he made one stop at the trading post for a few items, and for one piece, in particular: an item that he had gone without for too long, particularly for a man that was being hunted by other men.

Chapter 16

Jane Montgomery was a handsome woman somewhere in her early thirties and the last heir to the Montgomery fortune. She was a widow by her own hand. In her early twenties, she had been married to an adopted step-brother by her father's choosing. Jane knew she had no choice in the matter and accepted the union, but the marriage only lasted for three short months. She shot and killed her husband and the prostitute, where they lay in the bed of the town's bordello. The trial was swift and with Montgomery money in the pockets of the judge and jury, she had been acquitted of the murders by her peers. She never remarried, and spent most her time helping her father run the family business, taking complete control after his death.

Jane's father had died in his sleep three years ago. In the past two years, her brothers Richard and Duke had been killed. They were both killed by the same man: a southerner, a savage half-breed—an abomination in her eyes. The Montgomery money was now hers and hers alone and she would use it to have her revenge against the man that disrespected the family name. The mental instability and sheer meanness that ran through the Montgomery blood was pumping strong in Jane. She had the intelligence of her father, the ruthlessness of Richard, and the heartless, crazed demeanor of Duke all rolled up into the spite of a woman's scorn. Jane Montgomery was known by those around her as Bloody Jane, a reputation that she had assuredly earned.

Richmond, Virginia, had suffered massive devastation during the Civil War, leaving it vulnerable for a takeover to anyone with the money to rebuild it. Northern money was there to pick up the pieces as Jane opened the first National Montgomery Bank of Richmond. She bought land and hired the workers to rebuild the city. She bought the politicians that would run it gladly from the seat of her pocket. Her money set the local paper back to work printing the daily news, but the first papers off the presses were wanted posters—one hundred of them—with the name Hunter James Dolin upon them. This set the horses running in all directions and reaching out-of-work soldiers that were now guns for hire.

John Duncan Riley had first worked for the elder Montgomery at a very young age and was a man to be trusted. There was no job he wouldn't do for the right price, and he was the first one to hold a half-breed wanted poster in his hands, placed there by Jane herself. Five thousand dollars was a lifetime of money for normal folk, and a high roller could live well for years; but for some men, it was not the money but the work. John Duncan Riley was one of those men. The job was more important than the money. So, when Jane offered him an extra one thousand dollars to locate and detain the half-breed, he decided to make a trade in its stead.

What Jane Montgomery really wanted was to execute the half-breed herself and if Duncan could capture and contain the gunslinger, she would come to him and pull the trigger, close and personal-like, face-to-face.

Duncan and Jane once had relations when she was very young unbeknownst to her father or her brothers. That would now be his price for a capture instead of the kill. Jane agreed to the terms of the agreement, and for an incentive, she gave herself to him that night as a reminder of the bonus to come, for killing the Half-Breed Gunslinger would be hard enough, but capturing him would be damn near impossible.

☐ ☐ ☐

Six months had passed since that night. Jane Montgomery stood inside the doorway to her Virginia home and read the letter she had just received as the carrier waited. Duncan was convinced he had found Hunter James Dolin's settlement just outside a small cow town called Myakka City. The half-breed was aware of the bounty, but he had friends, and it appeared that he would not run. Duncan would do nothing until she gave the word. If she still wanted him alive, she would have to bring armed men with her. There was a p.s. under Duncan's signature that told of a woman and a small child that were family to the half-breed. Jane replied with a letter of her own and paid the carrier extra to assure a quick delivery.

It took a week to gather and prepare for the journey south. Jane traded her fine dress for pants and carried a set of Colt .45's that she had mastered at a young age, trained by her father. Five well paid gunmen accompanied her on horseback, and two of her Negro hands drove the wagon of supplies as they started the trek to the swamps of Florida. In Jane Montgomery's mind, they were going there to set things right.

Chapter 17

Days and weeks went by which turned into months, and all had been quiet at the cabin. Little James was growing and already getting to his feet. Alameda was raising the boy in the ways of the Indian. The Seminoles raised their children like the animals did in the wild; the sooner they could set their feet, the less vulnerable they were to predators. Helen understood their methods and Hunter absolutely did, for he was raised by the Seminoles as a young child. Mocha never left little James's side, "like they were stuck together with horse glue" was the saying that brought smiles to the mother and father. Alameda would grin once in a while, but only when she was with the child, never in front of the child's parents.

Mocha even enjoyed hauling little James around on her back in his horse training. This was common practice as young Indian braves of the Miccosukee would ride dogs and young pigs, bareback and holding the scruff of the neck or the ears of the squealing pigs, until they were big enough to climb on the back of a horse. Mocha did not enjoy the pulling at her hair, so Hunter made a blanketed saddle to fit the dogs back with straps of leather for the child to hold. The boy was a natural, and would play and ride Mocha under the big oak tree daily.

Today was hot and windy and pushing into the afternoon when Hunter sensed a presence, a feeling that they were being watched. He and Helen were blue crabbing near the fork where the creek branched off from the main river. Here, the water was slow-moving and the big blue crabs hung around at the deep part at the drop off. He said nothing to Helen and showed no sign that anything was wrong as he observed the landscape for any movement. He saw nothing; but someone was there, and he knew it deep in his bones. Hunter stood, slow, and stretched.

"I'm gonna call on the outhouse."

"Hurry back," she answered. "You're much better with these crab lines than I am."

Hunter bent down and kissed her cheek and then whispered in her ear looking as if he were kissing her neck.

"We are bein' watched from a distance, be on your guard."

Hunter walked toward the side of the house where the small dump shed was built off of the outer wall. He could open the door and then slip around to the front of the house appearing to have entered the dump shed which is what he did, circling around and entering the cabin unseen. On the table sat the new looking glass he had purchased in town. The merchant had called it a telescope. He extended it open and went to the back window where he began to scan the woods past Helen and across the river. She was sitting on the downed log and checking the grab lines, but he knew she was watching the woods for movement.

Hunter slowly panned across the thicket when he spotted a man well-covered and facing where Helen sat. The man stood and left the area, giving Hunter one good look through the trees to see it was the man called Duncan. Jeb and Walt had described the man, and he had no doubt that this was him. Hunter was convinced Duncan had been watching them for some time, and if the bounty hunter had not made a move it meant he was waiting for something; more men, most likely.

The gunslinger opened the door on the outhouse and allowed it to slam shut as he walked down to the river. Helen gave him a smile as he sat down next to her. He studied the spot where Duncan had been holed up, and he had the feeling the man had gone.

"What's goin' on, Hunter? Talk to me."

"Bounty hunter keeping track of our whereabouts." Helen's hand went to the butt of her gun. "Easy, woman. He's gone for now, but he will be back—and with friends."

"What'll we do?" she asked calmly.

"We can't stay here, it's too open. We could hold them off inside the cabin, but for only so long. Eventually, they would burn us out. Myakka City is where our friends are; they'll increase our numbers."

"Then we'll git little James, Alameda, and Mocha and go to town at once."

"It ain't safe for the boy or you. I think maybe you should take little James and go with Alameda to the Seminole tribe lands..." Before he could finish, Helen was on her feet and shaking her head.

"I will not stay with that Sam Jones. Alameda can take little James and Mocha out there, but I will go where you go." She turned and began walking up the bank to the cabin. "We best git packin'."

Hunter knew Helen meant to stand firm on her decision and there was nothing he could say to change her mind once she had made it up. The boy would be safest with the tribe, and Helen's skill with the gun would be handy. She had been battle tested and had killed without prejudice. She would be more dangerous now that she was a mother, like a mamma bear protecting her cub.

Hunter could not help thinking of what Jebidiah had said about Helen going up against the Montgomery woman. As far as he could tell, fate was heading in that direction. He made up his mind then and there that he would kill the Montgomery woman, if he must, to save Helen—even if it meant he would hang from the tight end of a rope.

Hunter walked Helen's path to the cabin to pack for the ride to Myakka City. As he crossed the grounds, a large black crow cawed at him three times from a fence post. This was the Indian sign for death. The crow was not telling whose death he was cawing about. Only time would tell.

The mental coldness to react without thought or conscience was a gunfighter's most valuable asset. Nerves of steel mixed with a deadly aim were the difference between a dead gunfighter and an old one.

Chapter 18

Little James was strapped on Alameda's back as she rode her bare back cracker pony. Helen rode Lady, and Hunter was leading the way with Zeke as Mocha followed. The dog followed from the side, the back, and sometimes took their lead. Mocha always looked back to check on little James and the others.

They had left the cabin in the early morning, two hours before the sun. Their heading was the Big Cypress Swamp and the Seminole Indian Clan, descendants of the Miccosukee and Lower Creek Tribes. There were eight known Indian Clans in Florida: Panther, Bear, Deer, Wind, Big Town, Bird, Snake, and Alligator. Apayaka Hadjo's Clan was the Snake Clan, for his name meant 'crazy rattlesnake'. No one knew why the white soldiers and the government called him Sam Jones.

They reached the village by late afternoon and were greeted by women and children running about. Mixed in were many Indian warriors surrounding them. The settlement was made up of many hogans at the edge of an unnamed lake that was at the entrance to the deepest part of the swamp alongside of the thickest part of the inland woods.

Hunter was concerned when he was not greeted by the chief, for not all the warriors revered him as Sam Jones did. Then again, Indians were a strange lot and could change their minds on a matter like the wind sometimes suddenly changed direction. More warriors closed in around them at the center of the village. Some had mounted their horses to meet the gunslinger face-to-face. There were ten braves in all, and the one in charge, Hunter recognized immediately—and it wasn't good. Hunter slowed at the front, Alameda and Helen did the same, side-by-side just behind him; Mocha came alongside Zeke and went to a sitting position.

"What is this?" Helen asked Hunter.

"Easy, Helen," Hunter replied, "but you be ready. Somethin' don't feel right."

Alameda sat quietly with no expression, even after Helen glanced at her with a questioning look.

Hunter talked directly to the man in charge, a young warrior that was poised to be chief after the death of Sam Jones. His name was Little Owl Tustenugee, and he was said to be the great grandson of Chief Osceola, the great warrior of the second Seminole Indian wars. Little Owl was young and arrogant and did not fear the curse of Lus-tee Manito Nak-nee; he had something to prove and the shaming of the gunslinger could help his status among his people.

"I seek the protection of Apayaka Hadjo and the Tribe of the Snake for my child," said Hunter with his hand up, the palm out and facing forward.

Little Owl stared at the gunslinger and said nothing.

Hunter pulled the tomahawk that the Chief had given him from his belt and held it up high.

"White men are waging war against me and I promise your chief a scalp from one of their fiercest warriors to hang on his hogan's lodge pole for all to see."

Hunter's words hung out there for some time before Little Owl finally spoke in a loud voice.

"Your Seminole blood is tainted by your father, Lus-tee Manito Nak-nee. I do not revere the old ways like Apayaka Hadjo. I do not fear the evil spirits, and when I am Chief of the Snake, *your* scalp will hang on my lodge pole for all to see."

Hunter's steel blue eyes narrowed as he pierced Little Owl with a look that filled the air with sudden tension. He spun the tomahawk several times and held it higher.

"You are *not* the Chief of the Snake People, Little Owl, not yet, and you will never be warrior enough to take my scalp."

The braves surrounding them began to holler at the insult, forcing Little Owl to pull his tomahawk from his rawhide strap.

"Keep your hands off them pistols, Helen. This won't take long," Hunter said without taking his eyes from Little Owl. His words stopped Helen's hands halfway to her guns.

The thundering of hooves from behind stopped Little Owl and the gunslinger from dismounting, as Sam Jones and the hunting party rode into the village and gathered around to face them. The chief yelled something in the Creek language directly at Little Owl. After a long and threatening gaze at Hunter, Little Owl turned his horse and rode from the circle. His anger was clear. Some of the younger warriors who seemed eager for a fight followed Little Owl out of the camp.

Hunter slid the tomahawk back in his belt and nodded to the chief. They spoke quickly as the sun was two hours from setting in the west, and as Hunter expected, Sam Jones still revered the power of his spirit. They spoke like old friends, with respect for one another. After a time, they came to an agreement.

Helen kissed and hugged little James and Hunter rubbed the top of his head. Mocha would stay behind with the child, with a promise from the chief that the dog would not be eaten, and that she would receive the same protection as the boy. Alameda was the godmother of the Clan and held much power that neither Helen nor Hunter had realized until now. She was properly introduced to Hunter and Helen by the chief. Hunter shook his head in disbelief. She was revered by her people, and Little Owl Tustenugee would have yielded to the wishes of this woman had she not just sat back quietly. Alameda was letting the men play it out, and Hunter and Helen wondered if she would have allowed them to battle, which would have certainly been to the death.

Hunter and Helen rode their horses hard and fast out of the Seminole village. The speeds they traveled made it easier for them to fight the urge to turn back. It was hard to leave the boy behind. Helen was especially struggling with the idea, but it was the safest place for their young son to be until their enemy was defeated.

Once they had covered a good distance, Hunter had slowed the pace from a gallop to a canter, then to a trot. Finally, he slowed down to a walk to give the horses time to cool down. During the walk, they would stop only once for the watering, and then start the run over again.

They walked the horses over toward a small pond. Hunter sensed Helen's stress. He dropped down from Zeke's back and helped Helen slide down from her mount. He wiped a tear from her cheek with his gloved hand.

"I'm fine," she said. "I just don't like leaving him."

"I know." Hunter handed her his cigarillo; she took a few puffs which helped to slow her breathing. "You have to channel that fear," Hunter explained. "You have to turn the fear into controlled anger, allow your survival instincts to take over."

"Yes," she said.

"Do you want to see little James again?"

Helen shot him a look. "Yes!"

"Then you must survive at all costs. Death is not a choice; kill or be killed, and do not waver. Do you understand?"

"I do understand," she replied sternly. "*I will not waver.*"

"Good," he said. "Your skills with a gun are only as good as your mind set in a battle, and now you will have both."

They watered the horses and then started another run, continuing on until they reached the road that led into Myakka City. They had made good time and allowed the horses to walk the last two miles, only stopping once at the sign that marked the cowtown. The new sign that Bodie and Bird had made was attached to one old post that simply read, 'Cowtown of Myakka'.

Hunter scanned down the sign post to where a chain hung from an old piece of wood covered in vines. He could see through the foliage where a number "6" was crossed out with a blade...*his* blade. The population of Myakka City had gone from 60 to 0, wiped out in one night in the first battle between himself and Richard Montgomery. *How many times would this place be destroyed by his hand?* he questioned. *As many times as it takes.*

"What is it?" Helen asked.

"Nothin'," Hunter said as he began to check his guns. Helen did the same. "Let's ride in slow, and keep our eyes peeled."

It was late afternoon when they started their walk down the road into town. As they got closer, the sounds of hooting and hollering could be heard, followed by gun shots, the cracking of a whip and then laughter. There was the music of a harmonica in the distance playing "Dixie", and the unmistakable squeaking sounds of bat wing doors swinging in and out.

They rounded the corner and all the sounds they'd heard could now be seen. Cracker cowboys were here, and the town was alive with drinking, gambling and games. There were working girls going from the saloon to the hotel and back; local gals—white, black, and Indian. As they rode in closer to the entrance of the saloon, the sound of clanking coins could be heard from the card tables over talk and laughter. The folks moving about the street became quiet when they noticed the gunslinger and the paint horse. The peoples in these parts had heard the legends of the Half-Breed Gunslinger, but most had never seen him.

Missourians had Jesse James; Tennesseans had Davy Crockett; Iowans had Buffalo Bill Cody; and Floridians of the southern swamps had Hunter James Dolin. The Half-Breed Gunslinger turned heads and pushed elbows in the sides of whispering gawkers. Hunter could feel the eyes upon him and when they entered the saloon, there was more of the same. The saloon went quiet for an uncomfortable moment and then the swinging of the doors broke the silence, sending everyone back to their business.

Hunter guided Helen to the corner of the bar, placing him between her and the patrons as Walt shuffled his way down to serve them. More glances came from around the room, and most were spellbound with Helen. They had all heard tales of Annie Oakley, but seeing a woman with tied-down guns alongside her pants and, at the same time, a natural beauty from her spurred boots to the top of her Stetson, was an unfamiliar sight to see.

"What can I git ya?" Walt asked.

"A beer, please, Walt," said Helen.

"Whiskey and a beer," said Hunter.

Walt gave Hunter a look, and then he turned to pour the beers. He turned back, looking around the saloon nervously. He set the beers down and pulled the cork on a bottle, then filled a shot glass and slid it to Hunter.

"What in the heck are you two doin' here, gunslinger?" whispered Walt. "You got a bounty on your head and now everybody knows where you are! Lucky there's only a few left in town—most moved on."

Hunter slammed back his shot and then searched around the room with a steady glance. The ones looking in his direction turned away. Hunter looked to Walt.

"The ones that really matter right now already know where I am."

"What's your meanin', son?"

"Duncan," said Hunter and then he sipped his beer. "He's been scoutin' the cabin for days, weeks maybe. He's made no moves."

Walt scratched his beard as if it helped him think.

"That means Duncan's waitin' on friends, maybe... waitin' on back up. Shit! Who you expect he's waitin' on?"

"I reckin' the Montgomery woman, along with more hired guns, most likely."

There was a long pause, and then Walt spoke with urgency. "We need to git the boys together and come up with a plan."

Helen put her hand on top of Walt's hand and squeezed. "Thank you, Walt. You're a good man. All of you have always taken care of me."

"Young lady, we're a family—and families stick together. Besides, we been through too much shit to lay down now. Anyway, I'm gittin' tired of them Yanks comin' down here thinkin' they can kick us around. This damned war ain't never gonna be over."

Bessie came in through the back with slabs of beef for two cowboys at the other end of the bar. She looked right at Hunter, and then nodded.

"What was that?" Helen asked Hunter with surprise.

Hunter was a little surprised himself and did not have time to reply to Bessie before she turned away.

"We—ah, ate together and had a little talk; very little."

"Maybe you should try the same with Alameda?" Helen said, smiling.

Hunter gave Helen a look, but before he could reply to her, Walt came up beside him on their side of the bar and whispered near his ear.

"I'll git the boys together at the hotel. You meet us there in a bit."

Hunter nodded and Walt left the saloon. Bessie took over for him behind the bar. She and Helen talked for a bit till they finished their drinks, giving Walt time to round up everyone for a meet.

It was two hours before dark when Hunter and Helen left the saloon and were crossing the road for the hotel. Suddenly, the sound of galloping hooves came from the north road into Myakka. Hunter and Helen were in the middle of the street standing side-by-side when the horses rode in, clearing the streets.

The posse was led by Duncan and a woman with a striking resemblance that Hunter and Helen recognized immediately. The horses fanned out and stopped in their tracks like the front line of a small army. They were thirty feet from where Hunter and Helen had slowly separated five paces from one another. They faced the posse, standing firm in the draw position.

The only sounds were the hard breathing from the horses and the movements they made stomping in place. Their heads jerked and tails twitched until they settled down from their run. The tension in the air was thick as all eyes were sharp and looking for any threatening movements. The distinct sounds of a horse-drawn wagon could be heard coming down the north road. This diverted everyone's attention toward the two Negro men behind the reins who stopped quickly when they saw the standoff at their lead.

Duncan was the first to speak. As he did, he was careful not to take his eyes from the hands of the gunslinger.

"You'd be Hunter James Dolin, the half-breed wanted for murder?"

"That'd be me."

"We're here to take you to trial for the murder of one Richard Montgomery and one Duke Montgomery under authority of the Governor of Virginia."

"Trial," Hunter replied. "There will be no trial."

"That will be up to you, Mr. Dolin," the woman

said with authority. "Do you know who I am?"

"You'd be the last Montgomery, I reckon."

"You're greatly outnumbered, half-breed," said Duncan sternly. "Spare the life of your woman and come with us, or there will be bloodshed."

"Yes, Mr. Dolin, think of your child," said Jane Montgomery while looking toward Helen. "A boy growing up without a mother...give yourself up, and I give my word no blood will be spilt here."

Helen broke formation and moved behind Hunter, forcing everyone's hands to the butts of their pistols as she walked five paces to the other side of him, placing her closer and directly in front of Jane Montgomery.

"The *first blood* to be spilt will be *yours*, bitch," Helen said calmly.

Jane Montgomery leaned forward and the two women stared down one another. Hunter recognized the look in Jane's eyes. She had the crazy, evil gaze of Duke Montgomery, but also the cunning of Richard. The talk was over, and Hunter decided to shoot the woman first, then Duncan. His draw was only halted by the sounds of swinging doors and then spurs clanking on wood. Bodie and Bird exited the hotel, followed by Jebidiah and Walt.

Bodie and Bird walked the street and settled in at Hunter's far left, Jebidiah and Walt faced off to the far right of Helen on the street in front of the steps of the hotel. Bodie and Walt both held at the level, long double-barreled shotguns, covering the enemies' left and right flanks.

The tensions eased a bit as the odds evened up, but Jane Montgomery's hires were ex-soldiers and hired killers; fear was not in their nature.

"You're still outnumbered by one, half-breed," announced Duncan, "and your numbers include a woman, two old men and a boy. As you can see, I bring nothin' but professionals."

As soon as Duncan finished speaking, the doors to the saloon swung open and five cracker cowboys filled the porch with rifles and shotguns at the right flank of Montgomery and her posse. Duncan was the first to slowly remove his hand from his pistol butt. The other gunmen did the same. They knew when a situation was not winnable, for they were, like Duncan said, professionals. Only Jane Montgomery had to be convinced to back off.

Jane's and Helen's eyes were still locked on one another and they were a flinch away from drawing their guns.

Duncan talked quietly, but with some conviction.

"Miss Jane, I'm afraid the tables have turned; now is not the time."

There was a long pause, and Jane's eyes changed from crazed anger back to the cunning intelligence that had kept her in charge in what was clearly a man's world. She eased up, un-wrapping the reins from the saddle horn and into her gloved hands as she spoke.

"I will give you some time, Mr. Dolin, to set your affairs in order, but we will be back to serve the bounty."

"You do what you gotta do, ma'am. And I reckon I'll do what *I* must," Hunter said with a tip of his hat as the Montgomery crew turned their horses and rode hard out of the town. The wagon took a wide turn and followed.

Walt breathed a deep breath and slapped his hat on one knee. "Ooh, doggie! That was too close. Okay boys, drinks are on the house."

The crackers hooted and hollered as they filed back into the saloon. Walt followed to give the order as Bodie, Bird, and Jebidiah circled around Hunter and Helen.

"What do you think, son?" Jebidiah asked.

"You heard her. They'll be back."

Bodie chimed in, "They will most likely wait till them cracker boys leave town and head back north, to even out the odds a bit."

"That would make sense," replied Hunter. "Bird, can you track them down and find out where they're holin' up without bein' noticed?"

Bird was nodding his head before Hunter could finish.

Hunter continued, "I don't want you takin' no chances. The last thing we need is you to be taken captive—or worse."

"I'll be in and out; they'll never know'd I was even there."

Hunter looked to Bodie. "You all right with that?"

"He's his own man," said Bodie. "Besides, the only one better in them woods than Bird, here, that I know would be you, and maybe an Injun or two."

Bird bowed up like a game rooster with a small grin shining with pride.

"Don't git cocky on me, boy." Bodie used an extended finger to make his point.

"I got it, Bode. It'll be dark soon; in and out."

Helen faced Bird and palmed his boyish face. "You be careful, young man." She hugged him tight. "Don't you git yourself caught or killed."

Bird's face turned red as he gave Helen a reassured smile.

"They won't be far. You got two hours, tops, and then I'm comin' after ya," Hunter warned.

"I'll be back in one." Bird ran off to the barn to saddle up.

"What do we do while he's gone, son?" Jebidiah asked Hunter.

"Well, I heard a rumor drinks are free today."

Helen gave Hunter a look.

"Don't fret, my lady. I'm on the verge of a plan, and I just need some whiskey to jar it loose."

Chapter 19

Jane Montgomery and John Duncan Riley, with their crew of hired gunmen, set up camp two miles north of Myakka City. The two Negro worker men pitched a large tent for Jane Montgomery some distance from the crew. Duncan had pitched his tent next to Jane's. It was much smaller, and only had room for a cot. The crew would sleep by the fire under the night sky as was their usual, but there was some complaint when the Negro workers set a cover over the back of the now-empty wagon. White men sleeping in the dirt with the bugs and the snakes while black men slept under cover did not sit well.

Duncan quickly snuffed out the grumblings by offering the men the wagon in trade for what the former slaves were being paid compared to the monies they had received for their participation in this lynching posse. The gunmen had a pocket full of silver with the promise of doubling up that amount at the end of the hunt. Bonus money was offered for the capture of the half-breed, brought alive to the feet of Jane Montgomery. Not one man figured on collecting the bonus, for they knew the gunslinger would not be taken alive. This game they played was always for blood. The complaining was soon replaced with stories from the war over tins of whiskey.

□   □   □

Bird had picked up the posse's trail just before

dark and now watched the setup of the camp from a distance, leaving his horse and moving in on foot. Horses often called to one another, and sounded the alert when there was danger. A good horseman knew their range of sense and hearing, and kept that distance.

Bird was in and out like he had promised as soon as he was convinced they had picked their camp location. The last thing he saw was Duncan sneaking into Jane Montgomery's tent as the men settled into their bed rolls, and the lone guard dozed on a limestone rock jutting from the ground.

□　□　□

Duncan ducked into the tent to find Jane seated on a small wood chair, looking into a mirror which sat on a small table next to an oil burning lamp. He came up behind her as she let her hair down and kissed her neck. She allowed it for a moment, and then she stopped him.

"You need to explain to me what you plan on doing now, Mr. Duncan."

He backed away in frustration and began to pace, inspecting the shelter.

"Your tent is very spacious." He picked up a scarf she had been wearing and smelled its scent; he then picked up a bottle of perfume, smelling it, comparing the aroma between the two. "You seem to have brought some luxuries from home."

"The half-breed was ripped from my grasp. And that woman—" Jane's teeth clenched as she brushed the trail from her hair. "Ten pieces of silver to any man that kills her."

"Even the likes of these men are not going to deliberately shoot a woman out in the open, which would be a hanging offense in any part of the country. Save your silver and kill her by your own self."

"I *will* kill her." Jane spoke with an evil grin. "I will kill her in front of the half-breed as part of his torture, and what of the child?"

Duncan turned to face her with a look of concern.

"I'll have no part in killing a child; a man has to draw a line somewhere."

Jane stood. She turned and put her arms around his neck and whispered in his ear. "You just find the child...and *I* will do the rest."

Duncan tried to back away, but she held tight and kissed his neck passionately, rendering him helpless. They tore at each other's clothes while dropping slowly to the matted cot.

▯ ▯ ▯

Bird made it back to town with only minutes to spare before Hunter would set out to look for him. Walking tall and proud, Bird entered the hotel and met everyone in the eating room around the big table. He told of what he saw, and everyone knew exactly where the camp was located by merely knowing these lands like the back of their hands. Bird also mentioned the apparent relationship between Duncan and Jane Montgomery, which most likely made no difference, but did make for good chinwag. If Duncan was in love with Jane Montgomery, that could possibly be used against them—but Hunter figured Duncan loved himself more than he loved her when it came right down to it, so he tucked that gossip away in the back of his mind to sit until needed.

Jebidiah had the floor while Walt poured shot glasses from a new load of whiskey that had come into town recently. Whiskey was just moonshine aged in oak barrels for flavor and color, and this batch pleased Walt, for it was aged well and went down smooth. Jebidiah paced, waiting for Walt to finish pouring before he spoke.

"We need a plan, 'cause as soon as them cracker cowboys head back to the north ranch, Duncan and Montgomery and their posse will be back here to burn this town to the ground."

"I'll be damned if I'm gonna let them destroy what we have built here," exclaimed Bodie. He stood up, pacing with Jebidiah. "This is the closest thing to a home and a family I've had—well, in a long time."

"Let 'em come," said Bird. "Ain't nobody been able to whoop us yet."

Helen spoke up next. "Maybe we should just leave and lead them away from here."

"That thought did cross my mind," said Hunter. "After what happened today, they would burn this town anyhow, no matter if we were here or not."

"He's right," said Walt. "They're gonna burn it to the ground, come hell or high water."

"I don't know what that even means—hell or high water—you old coot," Bird replied with annoyance. "We know what they're gonna do; what the heck are *we* gonna do about it, is the question?"

Hunter leaned forward in his chair and snatched up a bottle. He poured himself a shot and slammed it back, then he lit a smoke. He waited for an answer to Bird's question from the others. When none came, he spoke his mind.

"We take the fight to them. They can't burn the town if they ain't anywhere near it."

"They wouldn't expect that," Jebidiah replied. "Their camp is on high ground, and they're watching the road that the crackers will travel home on, so they should sit tight until then."

"Then we got us a problem," said Bodie.

"What do you mean?" asked Bird.

"The cowboys' talk is they're headin' out tomorrow. Their purses are light, and the cattle trains are due in a couple-a weeks at the Florida-Georgia border."

"I can take care of that," said Walt. "Them crackers got plenty of time to git to the Florida-Georgia line. Free whiskey and women will git us a couple of days, and we can send them on a different road."

"We only need one day and part of the night," said Hunter. "The sooner we attack, the least they will expect. Agreed?"

All agreed they must take the fight to the enemy for the advantage it would give. This time, there was much more than just their lives at stake; there was the child to think of, and the town of Myakka that was their home. The Dolin Family was made up of mutts and misfits that had found one another after a time of separation and civil war, and they would not allow anyone to destroy what they had built without a fight.

The gunslinger was the leader of this rabble, and he set each one a job to do. Guns were cleaned and oiled, and ammunition was counted, stocked, and secured. Saddle bags were packed with jerky and sugar cubes which made quick energy for the horses, with only small amounts of grain. Double rations of fresh water and whiskey were essential for drinking as well as antiseptic for bullet wounds. Helen and Bessie stripped cloth for bandages and cotton for packing to stop any bleeding. The horses' shoes were checked and fixed, and all saddle straps and gear were gone over and repaired. Everything that could fail was checked and double-checked, for when going into battle, an army was only as good as its equipment and preparedness.

The enemy was not far and the battle would most likely only last minutes, but as in all confrontations, anything could happen. An ambush did not always work; getting caught in a cross-fire was always possible, depending on the plans of the enemy. Trapped or pinned down was always a possibility with injuries that would not allow a retreat. Most importantly on Hunter's mind was not allowing Duncan and Jane to escape. He and his soldiers would chase and hunt them down for however long it took. John Duncan Riley and Jane Montgomery must be killed and buried deep in the swamp to never be heard from again. Everyone in the Dolin Family knew this must be done if any of them were ever to live on in peace.

Walt's horse and supplies were taken care of by the others, as his job was to keep the cracker cowboys in town with a steady flow of whiskey. The working girls sat on laps and hung on arms. With vouchers for gambling, this kept the cowboys in town a bit longer. The cowboys knew they were being used for their numbers of deterrent, but after some discussion, they decided to play along. The head of this small crew made it clear to Walt that he had the rest of the night but they would head out the next evening as their job would require. It would be all the time needed to keep Jane Montgomery and her gunmen in their camp.

The Dolin Crew worked through the night and, with guard shifts, they slept during the next day and would head out that next evening in front of the cowboys who gladly traveled home by a different road, keeping their departure secret. The crackers

were southern boys and did not take kindly to northern thugs forcing their way into their territories,
especially after a bloody war. The defeat of the south
still soured in the bellies of such men, and would for
a very long time. The Half-Breed Gunslinger was a
legend in these parts and was more a brother to
them than any Yankee, regardless of his savage
blood. Most importantly, the crackers were loyal to
Myakka City, the only stop between the Tallahassee
and Key West cattle drives. They wanted the town to
stand for the fornicating, gambling, and drink.

Bessie prepared a big meal for all. Skillet fried
swamp cabbage from the hearts of palms, mixed in
with Walt's dry box smoker pork butt, marinated
beforehand in apple pie moonshine. There was corn-
bread and apple bacon fritters for dessert. They all
ate at the hotel, drinking whiskey moderately. They
did not speak it aloud, but they all looked into their
plates as if it could be their last meal. If they lived
through the battle that must come, there was no
telling when the next sit-down meal would be. The
battle would most likely be over that night, but if a
hunt ensued, it could be weeks. They would chase
their enemy clear to Georgia if need be.

After the clearing of the dishes and the last dis-
cussions of the battle plan, they would sleep. The
next day, they would lock up the town and head out
just after dark. Hopefully, the arrogance of Duncan
would keep his crew in wait at their position looking
for the departure of the cracker cowboys on the
north road. The cowboys agreed to leave by the south
road and give a wide berth before heading north. If
Duncan had sent a man out to watch the town, all
the advantages of a sneak attack would be for
naught, and Hunter and his group could suffer great

losses. Hunter was confident that the short time between their confrontation in town until tonight would not have been enough time for Duncan to have sent a lookout already. Also, knowing that he was occupied with the courting of Jane Montgomery assured his thoughts. The affair between the two was an advantage that he hoped would buy them some time.

Bird took the lead with Hunter, then came Helen, Jebidiah, and then Walt, with Bodie at the rear. Bird took them on the same route as he had taken the other night to the clearing just out of a horse's ear shot of the camp.

They dismounted and tied the horses. Hunter studied the camp through his eye glass from several different positions. He could see the men were finishing up supper by a fire and a guard was posted between them and the camp within rifle distance. The two Negro men had their own fire by the wagon; they were unarmed, and would not be targets as long as they stayed out of the way. There was no sign of Jane Montgomery or Duncan.

The gunman's horses were corralled behind the wagon and Hunter could not get a count from his position, so he'd have to assume Duncan was calling on Jane in the big tent. Hunter told all to be ready to move. As soon as the men in camp settled down for the night, he would go in first, quiet-like, and take out as many with the Bowie knife as possible. The others would spread out and circle just inside the edge of the woods and wait for the signal, which would be the first gunshot.

Hunter wanted to move around to the back of the camp for a count of the horses. It bothered him that there was no sign of Jane Montgomery or Duncan.

The men had been unmoving for some time around a diminishing fire, and the guard was already sleeping at his post.

Hunter made his decision that the time was now, and he pointed to each one of his group to begin the movement forward. He gazed at Helen. She stared back at him, saying much without words. Hunter pulled his Bowie and slipped silently into the thicket—and he was gone. The others moved laterally, spreading out to their positions, giving the gunslinger time to do his work—but they would be ready when that first shot rang out. Helen moved quicker, for her job was to circle around behind the horses and cover the back for any runners who tried to escape.

The blood seeped over the half-breed's clenched fist that held the knife as Hunter buried it to the hilt in the side of the sleeping guard. The mumbles were short under the other hand that covered his mouth. The rock the guard sat upon turned red and sticky, as blood poured from his lower side while the blade destroyed the kidney. Hunter laid the dead man behind the rock and moved forward like a bobcat stalking its next meal.

Duncan had made a huge mistake by corralling the horses behind the wagon far away from camp and not allowing their keen hearing to warn off pillagers. Hunter came into the clearing by the fire where the four men were bedded down. He went to the closest one and raised his knife, preparing to plunge it into his head. Just then, a shot rang out and a bullet whizzed by Hunter's ear. The man woke and grabbed Hunter's foot and took him down as the other men were getting to their feet and pulling their pistols.

Hunter tussled with the man and quickly rolled him on top using him as a shield as the others fired; the man's body took all the bullets in the back. At that moment, Bird, Bodie, and Jebidiah appeared from the edge of the woods with their guns blazing. Hunter rolled the dead man off him and got to his feet with his pistol pulled and ready to fire; there was no one left to shoot, for all four men were dead. Walt walked into the clearing with his gun drawn.

"Nice a' you to join us, old man," said Bird as he spoke over the clicks and sounds of each man reloading their pistols.

"Shush up, Birdie boy. I needed to take a leak."

"Well, that worked like a charm, gunslinger," Jebidiah said with surprise. "Not as planned, but I'll take it."

Hunter nodded with approval and then headed over in front of the big tent. Bodie followed him and they both stood on either side of the flaps with guns drawn. Bird went to the front of the small tent with Jebidiah, and Walt covered both tents from a distance with his revolvers cocked and leveled in between the two. Hunter nodded at Walt who stood ready as they all went in both tents quickly. Walt's eyes went from one tent to another as they entered. All was quiet until Jebidiah yelled out to Walt from the small tent.

"We're comin' out, Walt."

"All clear. Comin' out, Walt," Bodie yelled from the big tent.

The four men exited the empty tents. There was no sign of Jane Montgomery or John Duncan.

As they gathered around, Helen ran up from behind the wagon, alerting them.

"Oh, boys, we have a problem. The horses that

Duncan and that bitch Jane rode are gone, and it looks like for some time now."

"Ya think they ran?" asked Bird. "Cowards."

"No, I don't think so," said Hunter. "They must have rode toward town as we had set out for here."

"Makes sense," Jebidiah replied, scratching his chin whiskers. "Duncan's got the guts for such a move, and that Jane woman—she ain't leavin' here without your head on a stick, gunslinger."

"Where's the two Negros? Did you check the back of that wagon?" Bodie asked of Helen.

"I did. The wagon's empty. They're long gone."

"It wasn't their fight," said Hunter.

"You want we should go after them?" Bird asked.

"No, let them be," replied Hunter. "The deaths of the Montgomery woman and John Duncan will end this, but they will not go down easy."

They gathered their horses and rode hard for My-akka City. The one place where they were trying to avoid a standoff would now be where the last battle would take place.

The roles in this fight had reversed as they now had the numbers and were chasing down Jane and Duncan. One difference was they did not have the papers making it legal—but out here in the swamps, "legal" had nothing to do with it. It was about survival of family and property and honor. An eye for an eye was the law out here.

After stopping first to do a weapons check, they walked their horses into town by the north road. It was quiet and Hunter had a bad feeling as they halted in the street. The saloon was to the right, and the hotel to the left. They were in the same spot where Jane Montgomery and her crew had confronted them two days earlier. Hunter and Helen sat upon their mounts at the center with Bodie and Bird at the ends and then Walt on the side of the gunslinger with Jebidiah next to Helen. They were looking around, up at the windows of the hotel and at the corners of the buildings and behind them, but there was no movement. There was no one there to greet them.

"What do you think, son?" Jebidiah asked Hunter.

"They're here. I can feel it."

Just then, the doors to the hotel swung open and Amos was led to the front porch with one of Jane's Negro men holding a shotgun to his head. Bird was closest to the hotel. He drew his pistol, pulling the hammer back, and aimed it at the black man who held the shotgun to Amos's head.

"Not the Negroes' fight, huh?" said Bird.

The sound of sliding leather and clicking metal rang out as the rest pulled their pistols and cocked the hammers.

"Easy simmer. Hold your fire," ordered Hunter.

Fear could be seen in Amos's eyes, but there was also fear in the gunman that held him.

"Let him go!" shouted Bird. He and Amos had worked together for some time, and become good friends.

There came a voice from up above, from the second story window of the hotel.

"He will *not* let him go," yelled Duncan. "He will be killed unless the half-breed surrenders."

"What makes you think I care about this man?" answered Hunter from the back of his horse. He had turned Zeke slightly toward the hotel. Bird shot a look at the gunslinger, not liking what he had heard.

"Maybe you don't care about *this* man, half-breed, but what about this woman?" Duncan moved out from the side of the window jamb so Hunter could see that he had a gun to Bessie's head. The black woman's eyes locked with the gunslinger's for a moment. Hunter's heart sank, but his poker face didn't show it.

"What do you want, Duncan?" asked Hunter.

At that moment, the Negro gunman backed Amos up and disappeared back inside the hotel.

"I want your men to drop their guns on the front porch of that saloon and go inside. You and your woman will stay put."

"And if we don't?" yelled Jebidiah.

"Then this fine woman, here, and your black friend down there will be the first to die." As Duncan said this, Jane appeared in the window. She grabbed Bessie by the hair and pulled her back in, out of sight.

"Let her come, I can take her," Helen whispered to Hunter. "I *will* take her."

Hunter looked into Helen's eyes; he still did not like it, but he knew it must be this way.

"Jeb, Walt, Bodie, Bird, do what he says."

"Shit!" said Walt.

"You can't be serious, son?" asked Jebidiah.

"I am, Jeb; it's the only way."

"I don't like it," Bodie said. "I'll go inside, but I'll be damned if I'm dropping my gun."

Bird rode his horse out of line toward the saloon and stopped in front of Hunter and Helen.

"Kill them all, gunslinger, you kill them dead."

Bird rode over to the post and dismounted, then entered the saloon. Bodie did the same, and then Walt and Jebidiah followed without another word.

Hunter's eyes didn't leave the second story window until Duncan and Jane left his view. Hunter and Helen dismounted and slapped the horses' hind quarters, sending them down the road and out of harm's way. They went through the checking of their revolvers making sure all the parts were functioning. They practiced their draw several times to make sure the pistols slid well in and out of the leather without obstruction. Hunter talked quietly with Helen as they did this; she said nothing and listened intently. She shook her head several times in understanding as he instructed her.

Duncan and Jane Montgomery slowly and carefully exited the saloon and walked into the street. They took the gunslinger's stance at a distance of twelve paces across from Hunter and Helen. Duncan faced the gunslinger, and Jane faced Helen. All eyes were shifting back and forth, and hands were hovering over the butts of their guns. There was a quiet tension building in the air.

"You call it," said Hunter toward Duncan.

"On three, then," said Duncan, and then after a moment he began. "*One... Two...*"

Three was never spoken as Duncan and Jane pulled their pistols early in a planned ambush.

At the first sign of movement, Hunter and Helen reacted in chorus; they both pivoted on their heels while drawing their guns and dropping to one knee, crossing their fire. Hunter's aim was at the center mass of Jane and Helen shot center mass above the belt line of Duncan. Duncan was firing on Hunter and Jane was firing on Helen; they did not expect them to drop; and their bullets whizzed to the side and just above their heads. Hunter and Helen slammed their palms on the hammers of their pistols and did not stop until the clicking sounds of their empty cylinders were heard. By aiming at the belt line at a low angle and upward, the bullets hit them in the chest repeatedly until Jane Montgomery and John Duncan Riley fell to the street, dead.

Hunter's plan had worked like a charm. He would have to live with the fact that he had killed a woman, but it was a burden that he was willing to bear to assure that Helen survived. The only witnesses were Hunter's friends and they would keep his secret. Any others that would not would be dealt with permanently. John Duncan Riley was dead, another bounty hunter killed by a very dangerous profession. Most important was the death of Jane Montgomery. There was no one left of the Montgomery family to seek revenge on the Half-Breed Gunslinger. The City of Myakka had survived another battle, which would please many.

Bessie exited the hotel and walked over to Duncan's dead body. She glanced at Hunter and he gave her a nod. The black women kicked Duncan's body twice and then spit on it before walking away.

Amos ran from the hotel's front door and out into the street.

"Where's the Negro with the shotgun?" Hunter asked.

"He had done run outta here when you killed that Duncan man."

"Did he see it?"

"No, sir, we heard the shots and then seen them dead."

"What about the other one? He run off, too?"

"No, sir, Duncan shot him to make the other do what he say."

Hunter waved Amos off and he ran to catch-up with Bessie.

"Should we go after him?" Helen asked.

"No, I doubt he'll come around here again, and he

saw nothin'."

Bodie, Bird, Jebidiah, and Walt met up with Helen and the gunslinger in the street. Jebidiah gave Helen a hug and Walt gave Hunter a pat on the back.

"The Montgomerys are finally over with, son, and Myakka City still stands. Maybe this is the day we can stop looking over our shoulders," Walt said.

"Don't git too relaxed there, old man," replied Hunter. "Them wanted posters are still out there. The ending of the war has left a lot of men with no other way to make a living; bounty hunters will be a problem for some time, I expect."

Bodie broke in on their conversation, "The woman's body needs to vanish. The gators will do the trick. Duncan is gonna git his very own plot in the boneyard, with a big-ass sign to ward off any others that might want to try the Half-Breed Gunslinger."

"You do what you feel is best, Bodie, and thank all y'all for bein' here to help," Hunter said.

Then he turned quickly, putting everyone on their guard. He looked down the south road and the others followed his gaze but heard and saw nothing. Then, she appeared, running hard with her tongue hanging. Mocha stopped at Hunter's feet and would have collapsed if he hadn't bent down and held her. The dog was sweaty and covered with dirt and clingers.

"Git some water, quickly!" Hunter demanded.

"I'm on it," Bird shouted as he ran off toward the saloon.

Helen bent down and stroked Mocha.

"What is she doing here?" As soon as Helen asked this, her face changed. "Little James is in danger; I can feel it."

"We need to gather the horses and go right now,"

said Hunter.

Hunter turned to Bodie. "Take care of Mocha. Git her out of this sun and don't let her follow."

"You go; I'll take care of everything here," Bodie replied.

☐ ☐ ☐

Hunter and Helen quickly retrieved their horses. They headed out for the Seminole Indian reserve where they had left their young son. They were both trying not to panic, but they knew something was wrong as they rode hard. Hunter's only thoughts were of little James and his promise to himself. *If anyone had harmed his boy, there would be a blood bath—the like that had never been seen before.*

Chapter 20

Hunter and Helen managed the two-day trip in a day-and-a-half, and their urgency would continue until their child was safe in their arms. They entered the rim of the clearing where they were met by Indian children running. The women and a number of braves followed as they rode toward the center of the village where the chief's hogan stood. They were met by Alameda, who exited the home of Sam Jones; she had a puffy red cheek and her eye was black and swollen. This immediately sent a bad feeling through Hunter and Helen as they jumped from their mounts and faced the mother of the village.

"Alameda, where is little James?" Helen said while holding her breath.

"He is alive, but taken."

"Who has taken him?" Hunter asked with clenched teeth.

"Little Owl and ten of his loyal braves use the child as bait to draw you out, Lus-tee Manito Nak-nee, for the purpose of a new legacy as the leader."

"Where is Apayaka Hadjo?" Hunter asked. "He would not have allowed this."

Alameda bowed her head as she spoke. "Apayaka Hadjo has passed on into the spirit world. His breath left him for the last time shortly after you left us, and I fear he was poisoned. Little Owl is now the Chief of the Snake Clan and he does not seek my counsel."

Helen began to pace in a panic as Hunter began

the checking of his guns.

"Where have they gone, Alameda?" asked Hunter. His steel blue eyes pierced hers to the point that she almost involuntarily took a step back. Alameda could feel the blackness consuming his heart as the seed of the black spirit overtook his soul.

"Little Owl believes he must slay you on sacred ground to secure his legacy. To kill the Half-Breed Gunslinger, the white man would fear him. To kill Lus-tee Manito Nak-nee, the native peoples would revere him, and this would assure that he would become the greatest Chief of the Lower Creek Seminoles since his grandfather, Osceola."

"Where is this sacred ground that you speak of? Quickly, woman!"

"To the south, deep in the swamps; a place you know, where Apayaka Hadjo gave you the tomahawk, the same clearing where our ancient ancestors once did sacrifice."

No more words were spoken as Hunter and Helen mounted their horses. They rode to the end of the village and stopped at the water's edge and allowed the horses to drink their fill for the three days ride would be done in less than two, only stopping to rest the horses.

Helen could feel the change in Hunter; it was seen in his eyes and felt around the air that he occupied. Helen was concerned for her man, but she would sacrifice his soul for her son and use the black spirit within him for the sake of her family's survival. Hunter James Dolin would have it his way, and nothing Helen could say would change that.

The horses had been watered and were on the move as Hunter's thinking was only of killing Little Owl. The love for his son was driving his hatred, which was even stronger than revenge. All the work done by the witch doctor to drive out the infection had worked, but the black heart had only been suppressed, for it was a part of Hunter James forever and he pulled upon it for his strength.

Helen and Hunter refused to consider that their son might already be dead, totally suppressing these thoughts from their minds. The plan was simple, rescue was the agenda; Hunter would go at Little Owl and Helen would go for little James. And they would kill anyone that got in their way.

They traveled day and night and only rested the horses just enough to start out at a steady run once again. During the down time, they ate only for strength, for neither parent could find their appetite. They did not speak, and only focused on the job at hand. Hunter smoked and sharpened the tomahawk with a select rock until it would split hairs. The weapon given to Hunter by Apayaka Hadjo had killed Richard Montgomery, and now it would be used to slay Little Owl.

Hunter and Helen dismounted the horses and checked their guns. They were one hundred yards from the clearing of the sacred ground where the chief known by whites as Sam Jones had given Hunter the tomahawk.

"Are you ready?" Hunter asked.

"Yes," said Helen.

"We go in without hesitation and kill everyone we see, always moving forward. I will go for Little Owl, and you search the grounds for little James."

"I will find our son and kill them all," Helen said with a calmness that Hunter understood.

Without another word, they headed on foot at a steady pace toward the clearing. The gunslinger could feel the enemy's presence as they got closer. Just then, warriors attacked from out of the tall saw grass on both sides of the path that led to the glade. Hunter pulled his pistols and began to fire the Colts. The bullets hit their marks, the bangs were followed by thumb clicks. The braves had attacked with knives and hatchets but they were slow and impatient and attacked from the front instead of the flank.

Two Indians fell as three rushed him from behind the fallen ones. Hunter holstered his left revolver to free up that hand; he slammed his palm on the hammer, killing the three and emptying the Colt. The last man cut into his arm with his knife on the way down. Hunter pulled the other pistol and continued to move forward, barely noticing the wound. He heard Helen's guns firing from behind him and it took everything he had not to look back. She would have to fend for herself, and he would have to let her.

Hunter hit the clearing to face Little Owl who was standing in the center holding a tomahawk and wearing his war paint. There were four warriors at his sides with rifles leveled. Two of the braves at Little Owl's side suddenly fell as Helen was firing and walking the circle of grass to the right out from behind Hunter. Bullets whizzed by Hunter's head, but his eyes never left Little Owl's. The two remaining braves fled and ran off into the saw grass, leaving their chief. Helen took out after them, reloading as she went. Helen was sweating in a slight panic as she knew the warriors were going for the child. She followed as fast as she could, leaving Hunter behind to deal with the new Chief of the Snake Clan.

Helen's guns were cocked and ready as she pushed through the chest-high saw grass. Her eyes were ablaze and her ears were focused on the slight-est sound. She suddenly heard a child's cry with the sound of movement up ahead. Helen picked up the pace, almost running. She broke through the saw grass into a small clearing at the river bank. An Indian from her left tried to club her with his rifle. She ducked and rolled and fired a shot into the belly of the brave. He went down and raised his rifle for a shot, but before he could pull the trigger, Helen put a bullet through his left eye.

She got to her feet and turned toward the rushing river to see the last Indian standing in the moving current; the water was up to his knees, and he held little James in his arms with a knife to his throat. The toddler's eyes were wide but he did not cry out. Helen raised her Dragoon and pulled the hammer back with her thumb. She aimed at the Indian's head. She said nothing, for it was clear what must happen next. They were at a stand-off, being perfect-ly still for what seemed a long time when the Indian flinched to back away. Helen fired, and a red circle appeared on the Indian's forehead. He fell backward, and little James hit the water with him. The current took the child as the dead Indian released him and they both quickly flowed downstream. Little James was moving faster than the Indian's body. The boy was rolling and bobbing and gasping for air. Helen ran to the bank and into the water where she then dove in to swim after her young son.

◻ ◻ ◻

The Half-Breed Gunslinger slid the tomahawk out and then dropped his gun belt to the ground. He pitched the sawed-off shotgun on top as he moved forward to meet the warrior chief. Little Owl took two steps, advancing in an overhand attack. Hunter blocked the hatchet as the steel heads locked. Hunter then kicked him with a boot to his mid-section and knocked him backward. With a spin of his wrist, the tomahawks separated and Hunter charged with speed and accuracy. Wood and metal violently met with high strikes, low swipes and side arm swings as they battled in the middle of the clear-ing. The Indian pushed back and then lunged with his shoulder, catching Hunter in the gut; they fell to the ground and rolled out of it quickly as they both rose to their feet, trading places in the circle of the grass.

Little Owl pulled his knife with his left hand, still holding the hatchet in his right, and slowly began to circle. Hunter reached back and pulled the Bowie knife from his belt. He moved sideways with his en-emy until they were back to their original position. Little Owl and Hunter attacked simultaneously with knife and tomahawk, and the dance was that of me-dieval sword fighters, attacking back and forth quickly. Both warriors were bleeding from their fore-arms from nicks and cuts, but so far, the battle was smooth-flowing and even. That changed when a shot rang out in the direction from where Helen had gone, and then another shot followed.

Hunter's concentration was interrupted for a split second, and Little Owl took advantage with a side swipe of his knife, cutting deep on Hunter's shoul-der. He winced as the tomahawk dropped from his grasp.

Hunter took a step back to see an evil grin appear on the Indian's face as he sensed he now had the upper hand. With the arrogance reserved for the young, Little Owl went for a death blow to the half-breed's head, but with the distance between them, it gave Hunter a chance to react. Hunter ducked and lunged forward. He put his good shoulder into the gut of the Indian. As he straightened his legs, he lifted Little Owl off his feet and flipped the warrior over his back and to the ground. The young Indian warrior got to his feet quickly and turned to face the gunslinger. To his surprise, the Half-Breed Gunslinger was now holding the shotgun on him.

"There is no honor in this, Lus-tee Manito Nak-nee," Little Owl said.

"You speak of honor—like stealin' a man's child? You're right, there is no honor in this."

Hunter shot both barrels, and Little Owl's bare chest opened up with the color of red as he flew backward to the ground, dead. He was no longer the Chief of the Snake Clan; he was no longer anything at all.

Hunter ripped the sleeve from his shirt and used it as a tourniquet, wrapping it under his arm, around his shoulder and tying it tight. He strapped on his revolvers and checked the ammo. Then, he reloaded the shotgun. He took off at a run toward the sound of the river where Helen had gone, which was the same direction from where he had heard the gunshot. *They best be alright,* he thought, for he hoped that there would be someone left to kill if they were not.

He reached the river in a matter of minutes and read the tracks at the water's edge. There was an Indian body snagged on a downed tree limb across the fast-moving river. Hunter could see it was one of the Indian braves that had fled. *Good girl, but where did you go?*

The only answer was downstream. Not seeing any sign of her and after quickly surveying the land, he made a decision to go back for the horses. If she was injured, the best place for her would be on the back of a horse.

The horses were well disciplined veterans and were grazing at the very spot where they had been left. With Helen's horse in tow, Hunter mounted Zeke and headed back. To Hunter's surprise, the bodies of Little Owl and his warriors had vanished. They were there when he passed by the clearing to gather the horses, but now they were gone.

He hurried his pace and rode the bank, heading downstream as the footing for the horses was good. As he passed, he looked to the tree branch in the river that held the dead Indian brave; the body had vanished like the others. An alarm went off in Hunter's head, knowing the Seminoles were about and collecting their dead, for he wasn't sure what their intent would be toward him. Indians were an unpredictable people and could change their minds as quickly as a flash of lightning from a storm forming in the southern sky.

After a time, the river widened and slowed but was also deeper, which concerned him. The bank leveled out and ran through miles of grass fields on the side of the river he traveled. The other side was thick woods and lower swamp lands. Zeke snorted and jumped as a water bandit left the bank and slithered across the top of the water to the security of the wooded side. Two bald eagles flew high and circled in the sky together as male and female, mated for life. A half-mile to his left, cracker cattle could be seen grazing, alerting Hunter that he was on occupied land; free grazing or plantation would not matter. The danger of Indians may no longer be a problem, but setting foot on cattle baron land could awaken a whole new set of perils.

The sun was becoming heavy in the sky, seeking the horizon. If darkness fell before Helen was found, it would hurt the chances of her survival. And what of little James? Where was he? Hunter was not a religious man but as the situation grew desperate, he began to pray as Helen had done around him many times before.

I know I have not followed any other path but my own. But God, if you can hear me, I call on you now to save my family from the evils of your world, and if you choose not to...

Before Hunter's prayer could take a wrong turn caused by a building anger, he spotted a form at the base of a large oak tree standing alone in the field of grass not far from the river's edge. He spurred Zeke to a canter and headed up the bank. As he got closer, he could see Helen seated and leaning against the trunk with little James held tight in her arms.

Hunter pulled back on the reins and slung his leg over Zeke's head and slid from his saddle all in one motion. He took three steps and dropped to his knees in front of them. They were both still, and their eyes were shut. Hunter's fear was at an all-time high until he saw Helen's chest heave with breath. Then one after the other their eyes opened; Helen gave him a weak smile.

"We're alright," Helen said in a steady but tired voice. "Just takin' a little nap after our swim."

"Pap," said little James.

Hunter gave them a rare smile. He removed his hat and wiped his brow with a sigh. He looked to the sky through the branches of the big oak. *Much obliged, Father; I shall never doubt again.*

"Was that a prayer, gunslinger?" Helen asked.

"More like a thank you than a prayer, I'd say."

The darkness around the gunslinger's heart diminished and retreated deep inside him once again, allowing joy to come forth. The blackness was not gone, but only suppressed, and would wait there until summoned. In this time and place, Hunter had no doubts that he would need the dark spirit of Lustee Manito Nak-nee once again to secure their survival here in the lawless lands of the Florida swamp.

About the Author

Bret Lee Hart, a second-generation Floridian, has spent the last twenty-five years in Marine construction; he is married and the father of two. His mother's maiden name is Emerson, as in Ralph Waldo, and on his father's side, Edgar Allen Poe can be found hanging on the family tree. With this bloodline of writers, and being named after Bret Harte from his western short stories, it was inevitable his imagination would find its way into print.

The *Half-Breed Gunslinger, Hunter James Dolin: The Half-Breed Gunslinger – Book II*, and *Montgomery's Revenge: The Half-Breed Gunslinger – Book III*, the first three books of this "cracker Western" series, as Bret calls them, are available in ebook and print at major online book retailers.

The Fangslinger and the Preacher is also now available and many other adventures are soon to be unleashed from this exciting storyteller's mind in various genres, including Fantasy and the Paranormal.

Be sure to watch for more titles from Bret Lee Hart coming soon from Sundown Press!

Follow Bret Lee Hart on Facebook
https://www.facebook.com/bretleehart
www.sundownpress.com

Printed in Great Britain
by Amazon